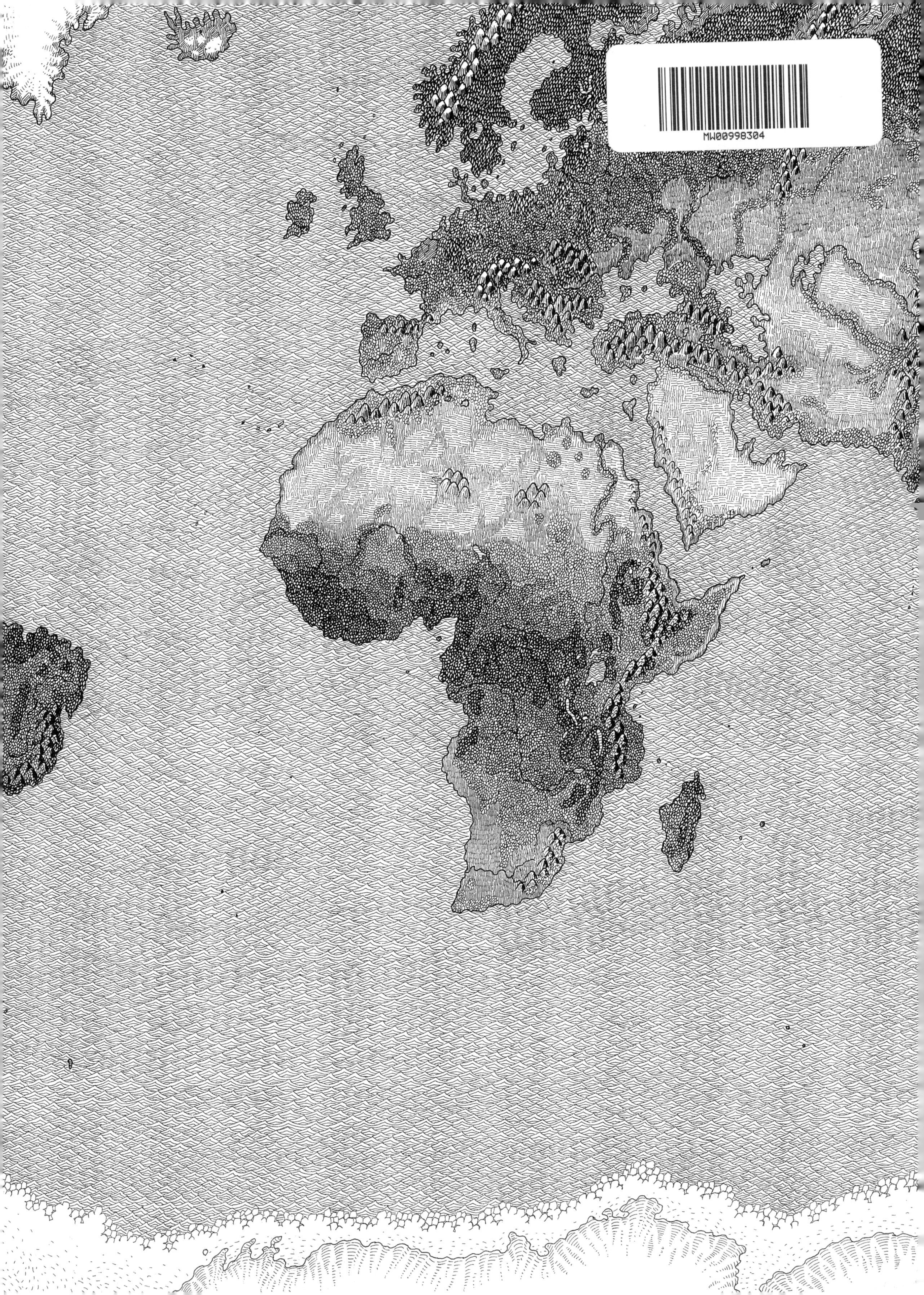

For Lune

This is an Em Querido book
Published by Levine Querido

LQ

LEVINE QUERIDO

www.levinequerido.com · info@levinequerido.com

Levine Querido is distributed by Chronicle Books LLC

Text and illustrations copyright © 2019 by Peter Van den Ende

Originally published in the Netherlands by Querido

All rights reserved

Library of Congress Control Number: 2019953569
ISBN 978-1-64614-017-6

Printed and bound in Italy

Published in October 2020
First Printing

Book design by Christine Kettner
The text type was set in Nicholas Cochin Bold

Peter Van den Ende created his illustrations using dip pens and Indian ink.
For more precision he used technical drawing pens.

PETER VAN DEN ENDE

THE
WANDERER

LQ
LEVINE QUERIDO

MONTCLAIR · AMSTERDAM · NEW YORK

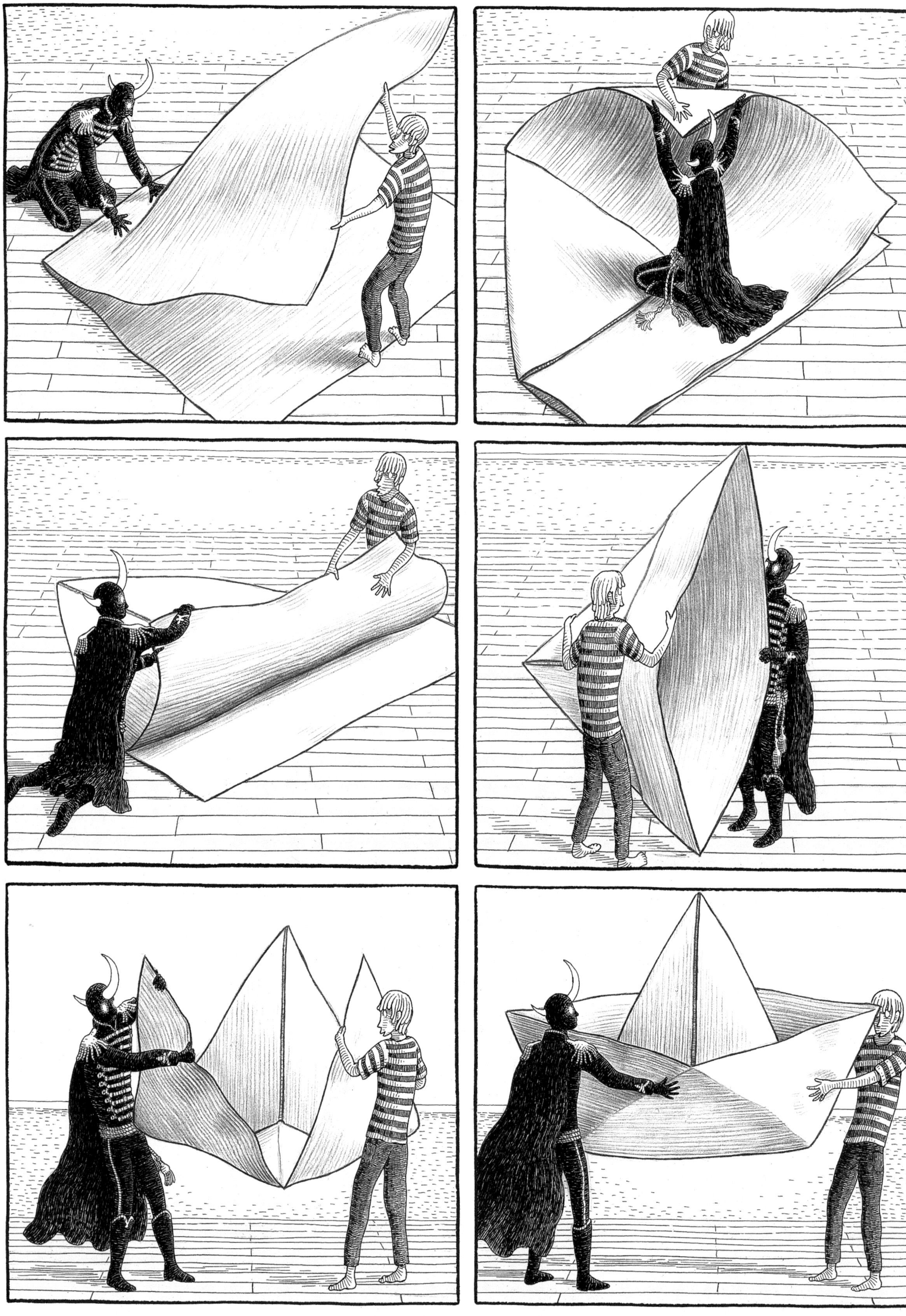

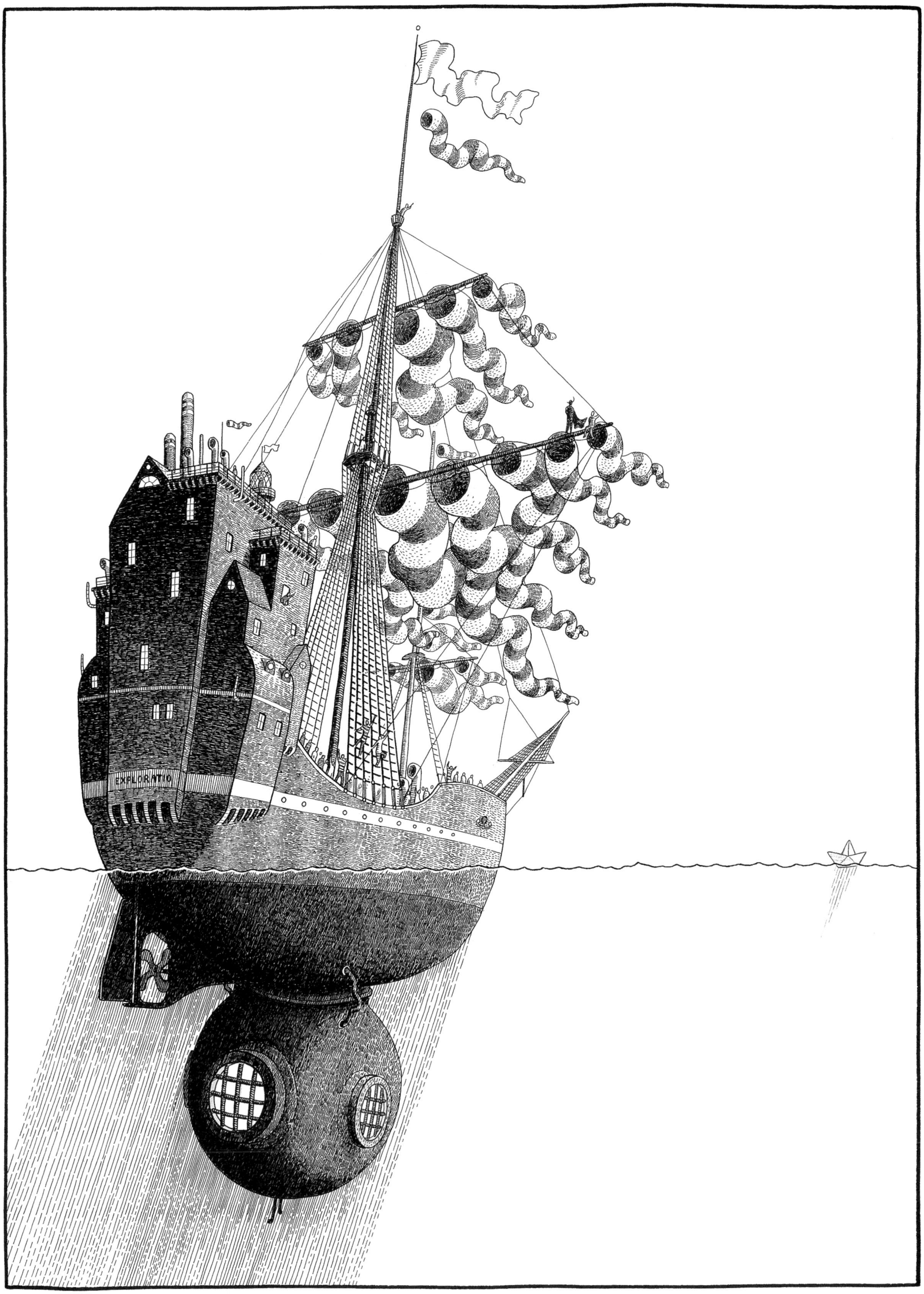
EXPLORATIO

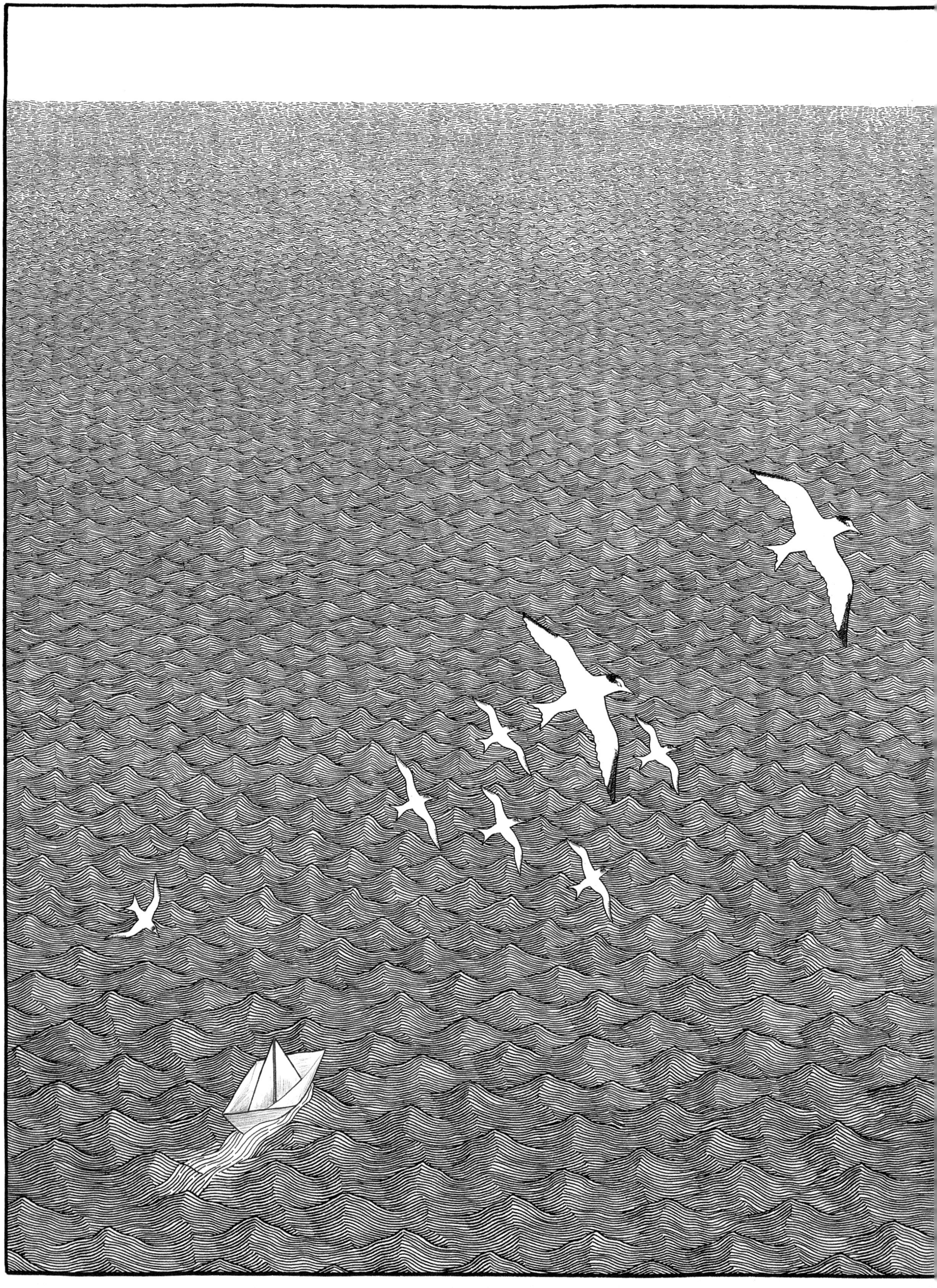

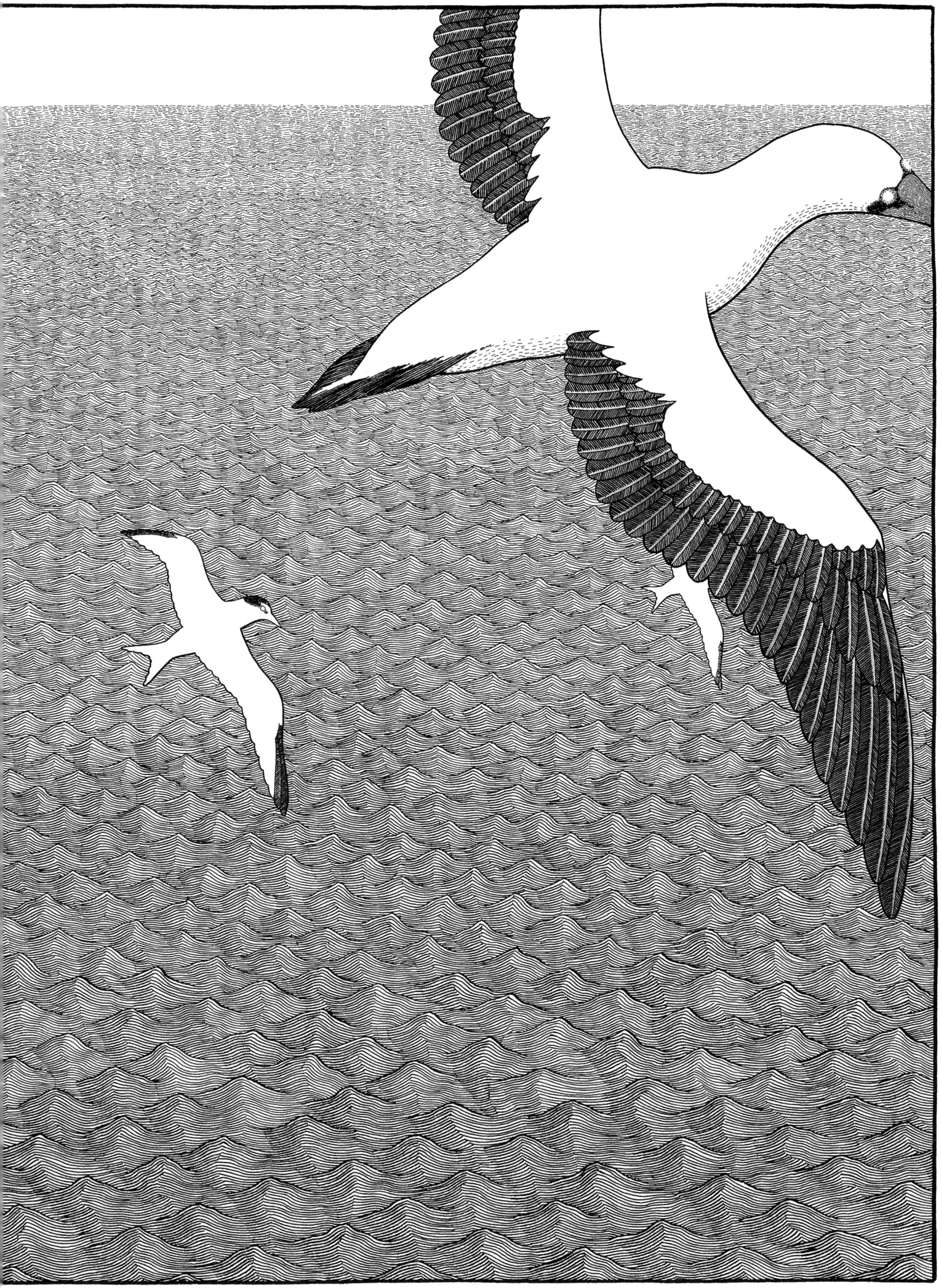

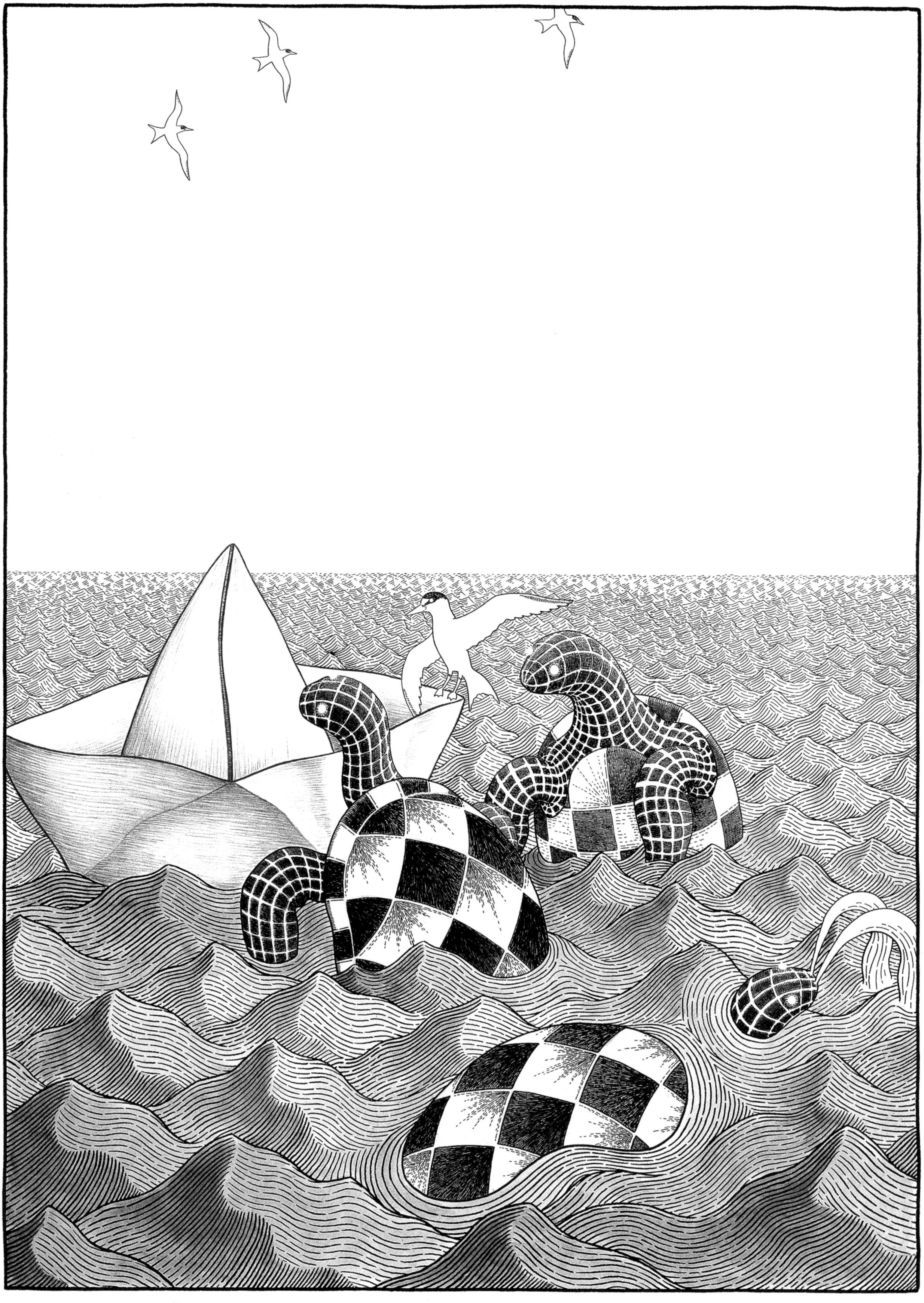

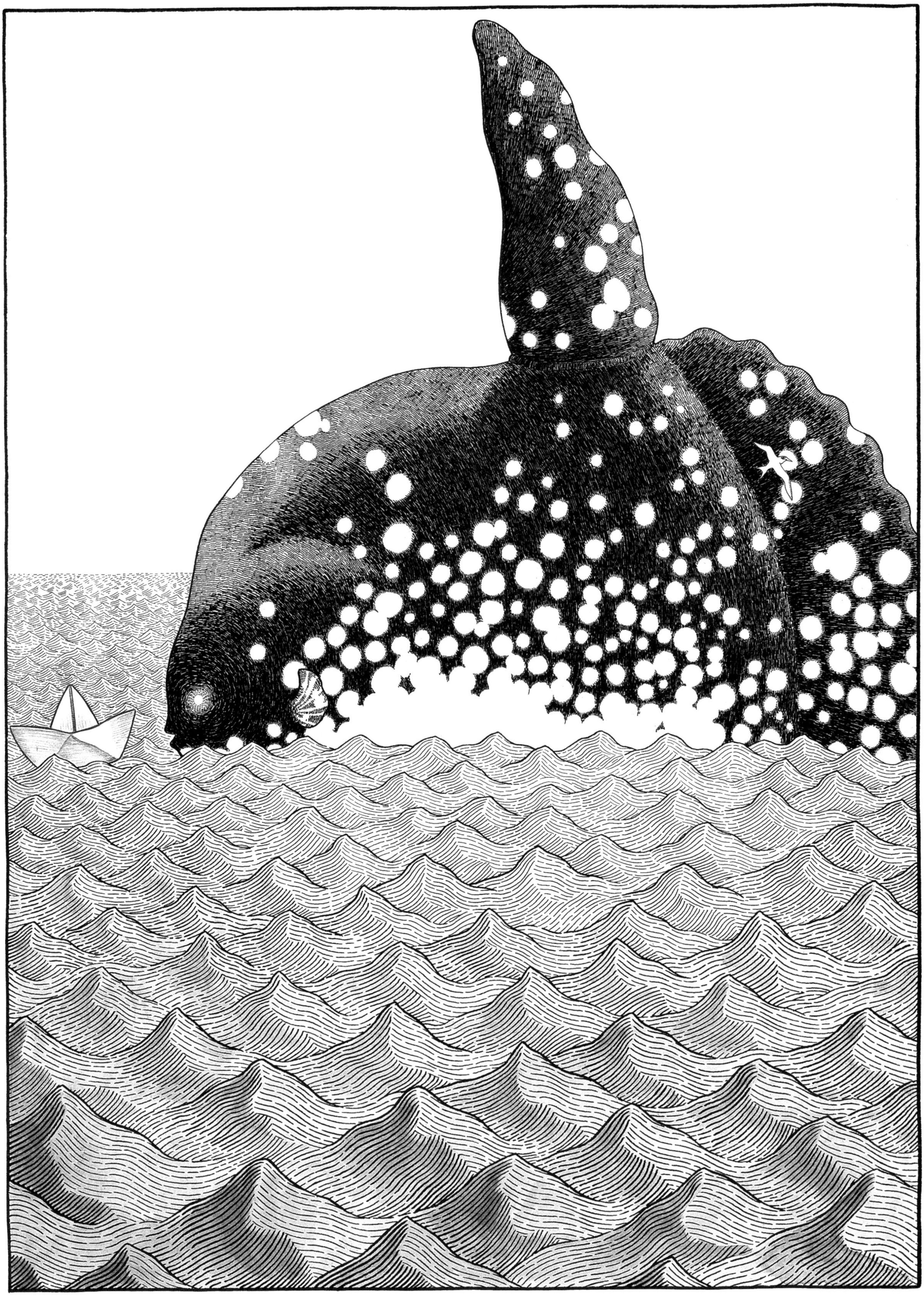

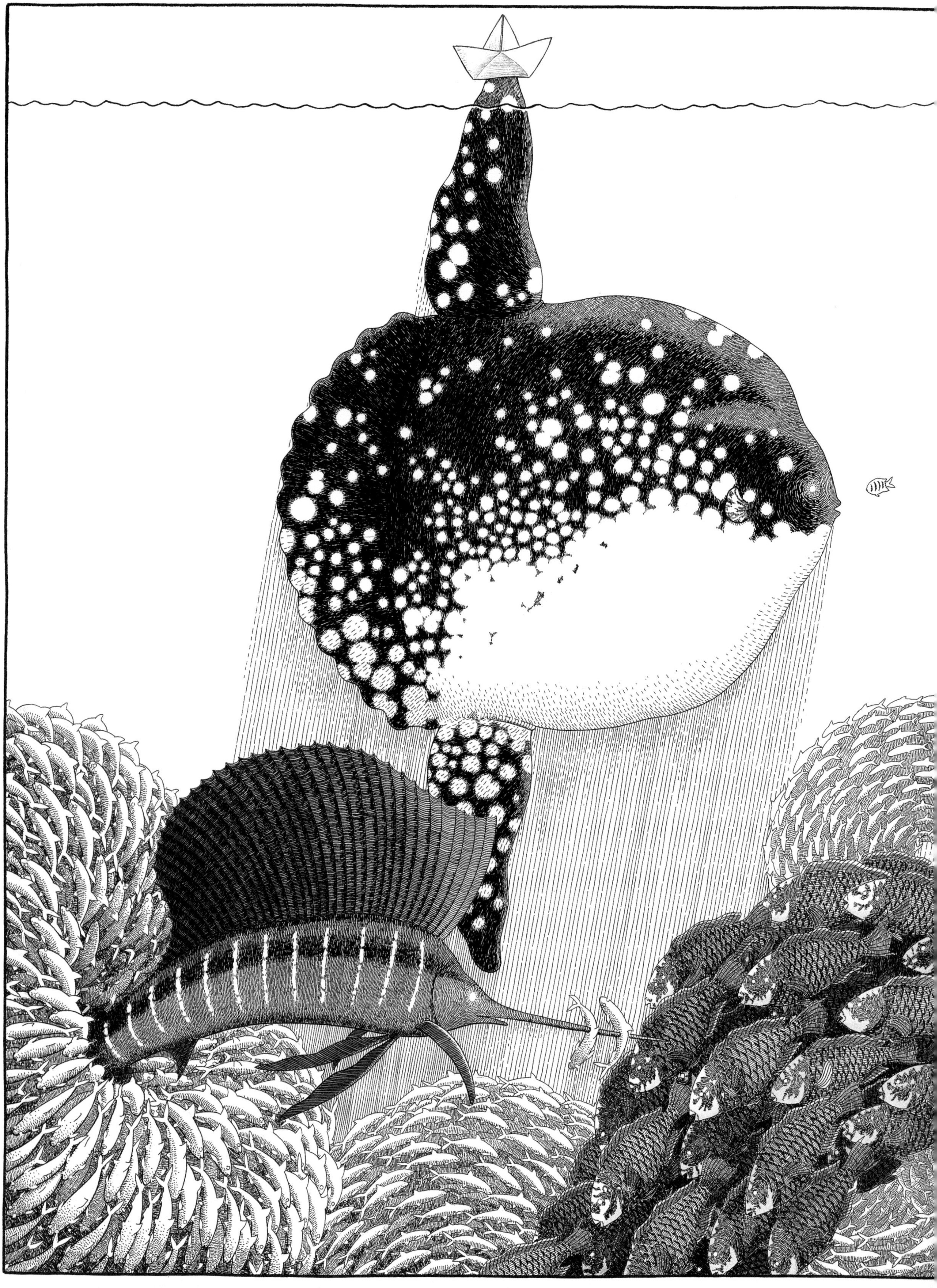

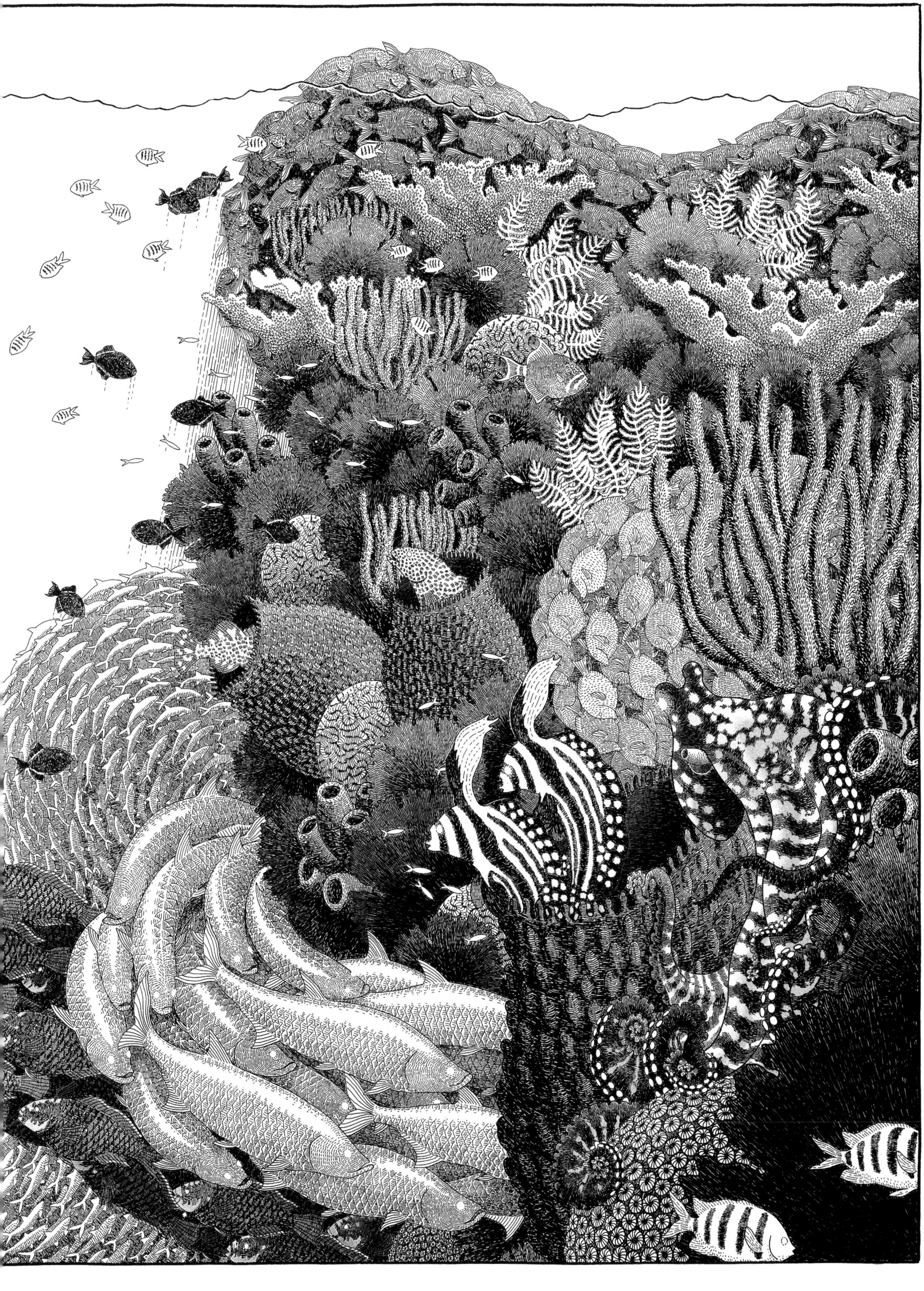

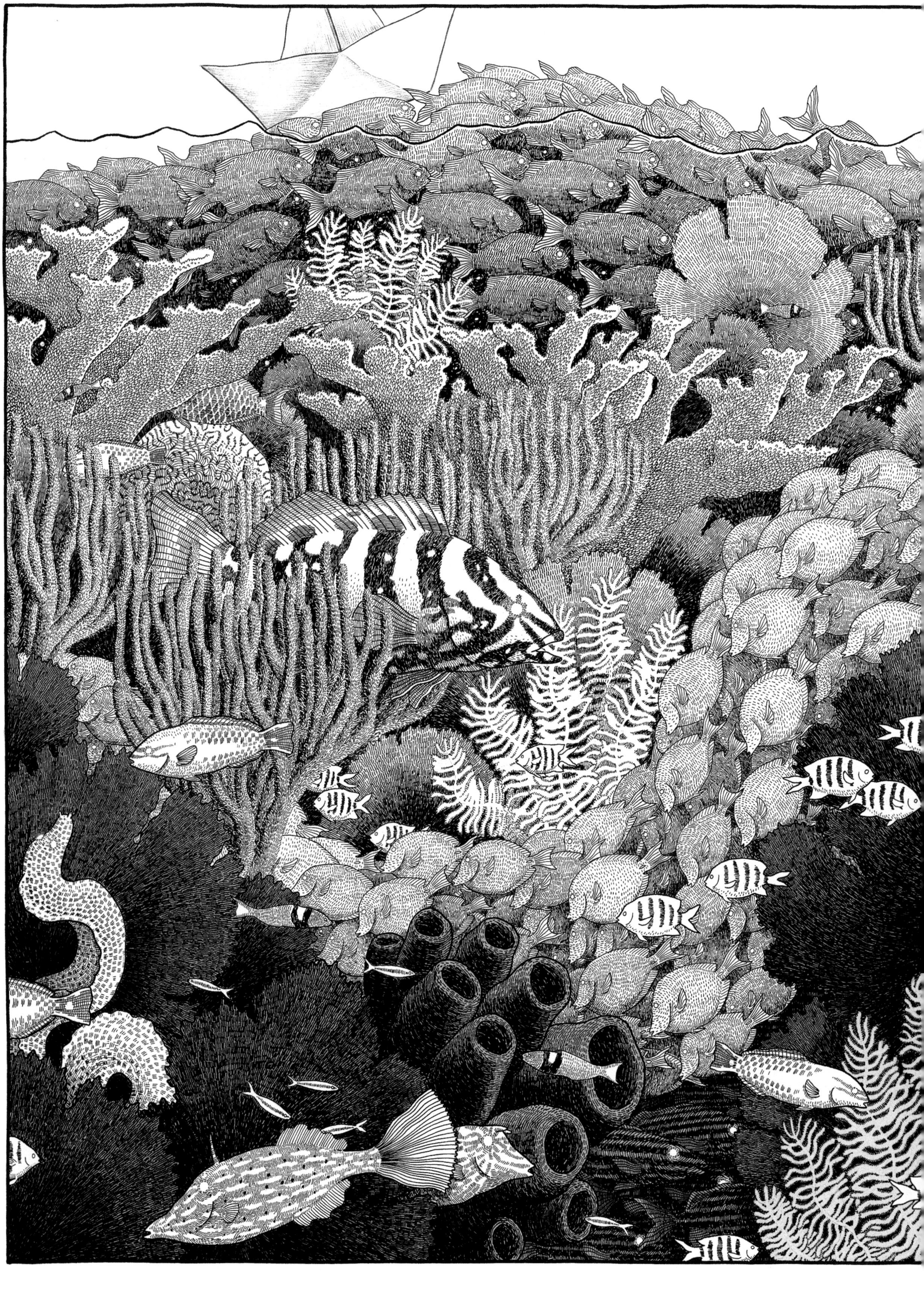

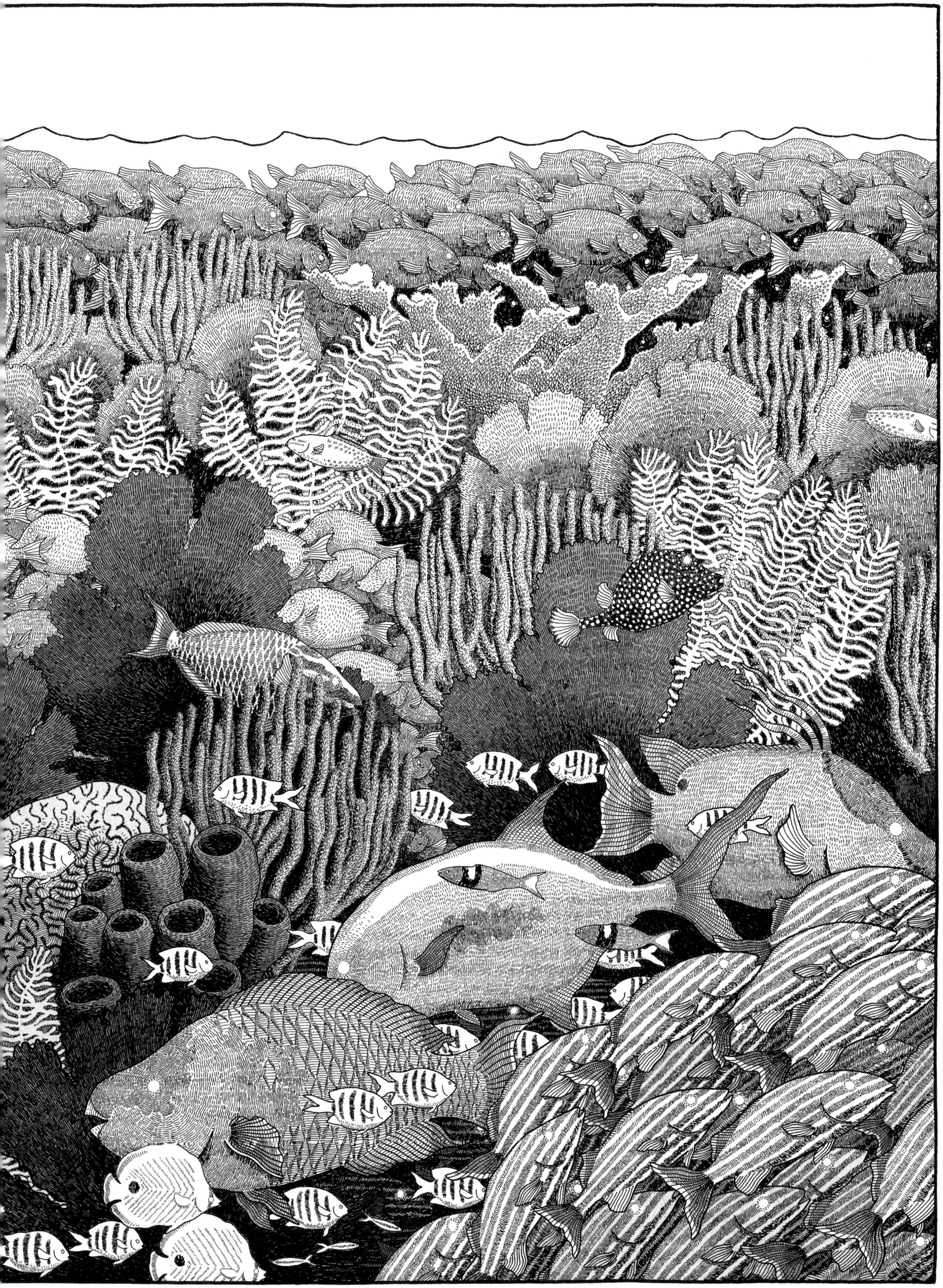

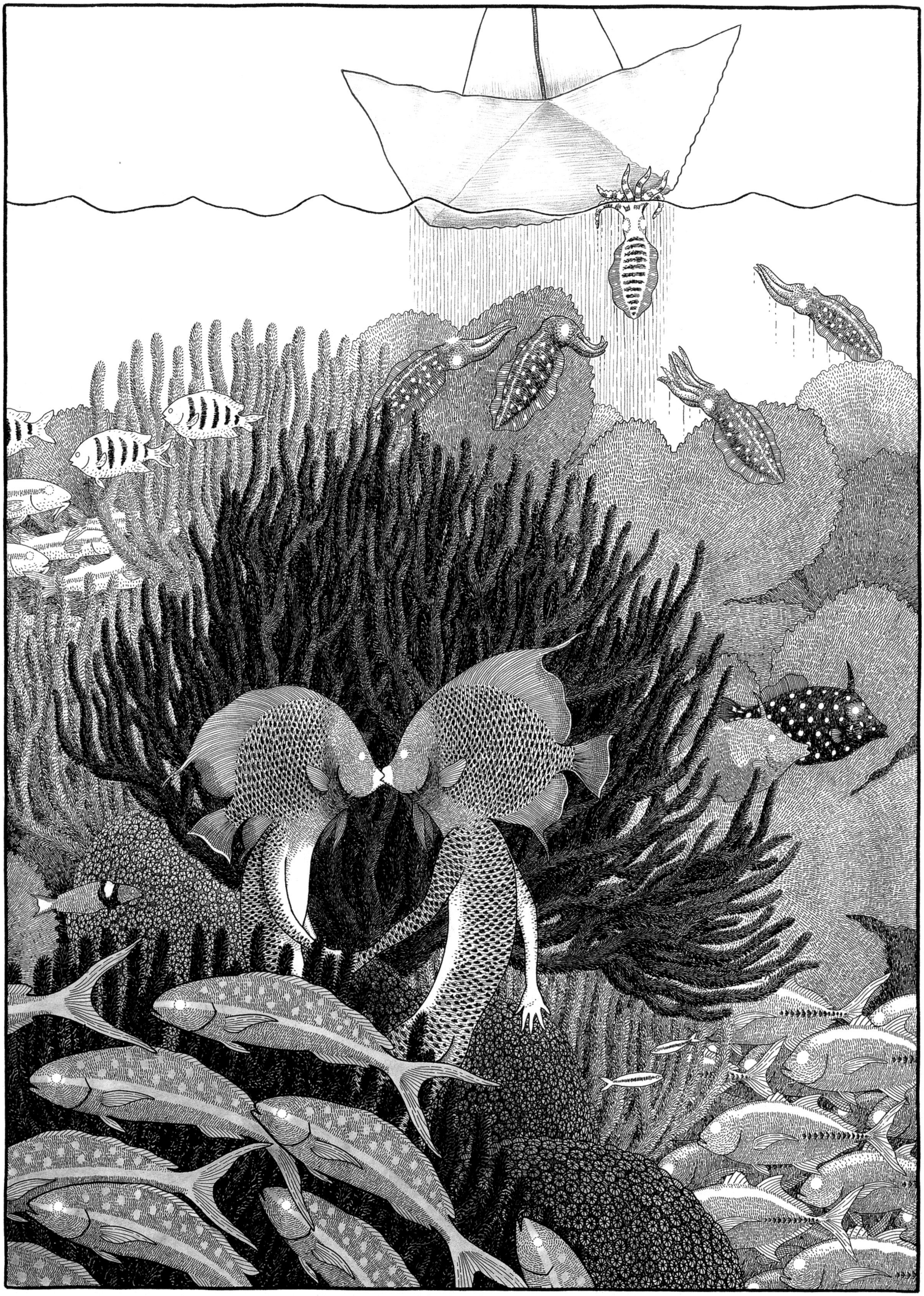

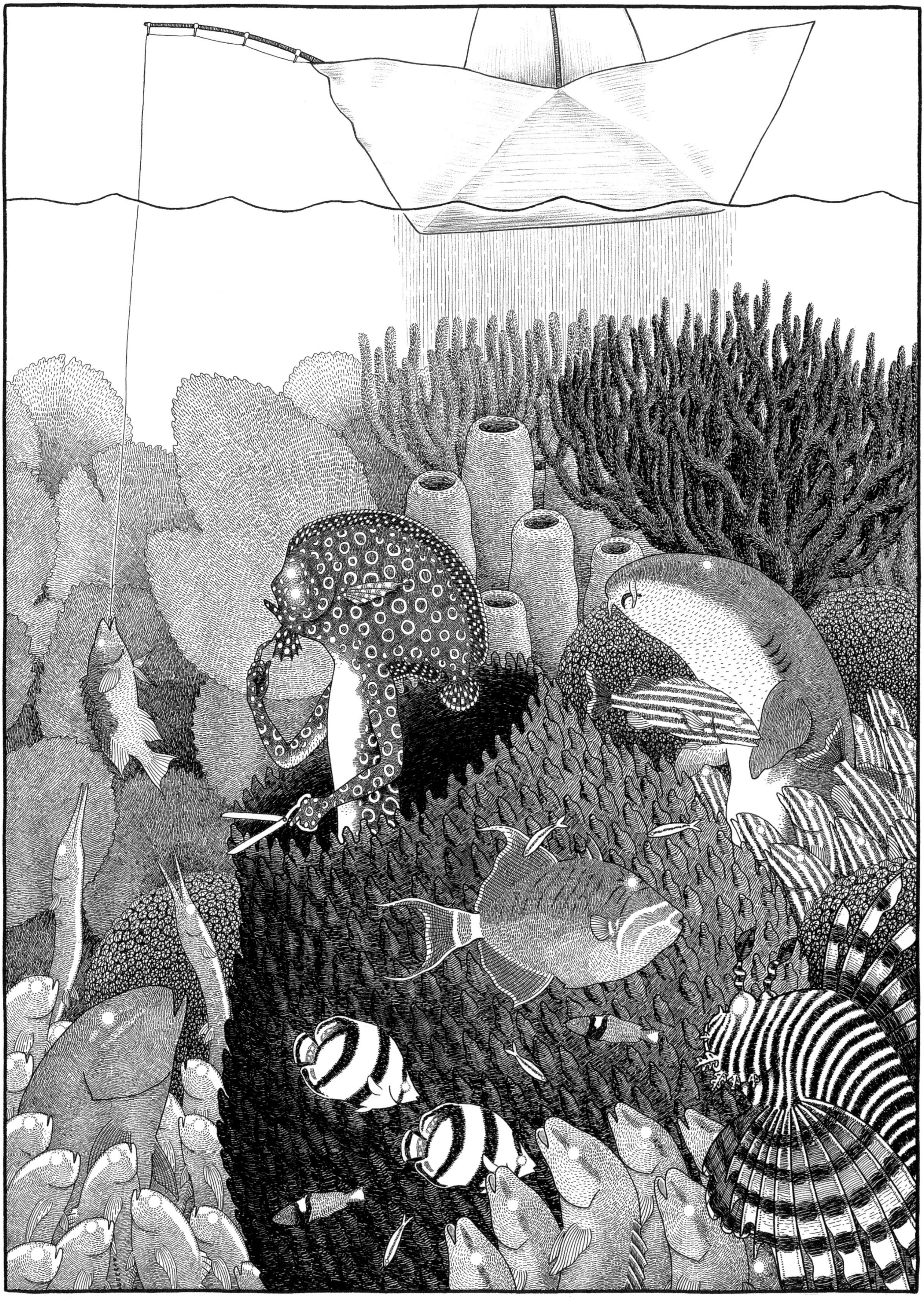

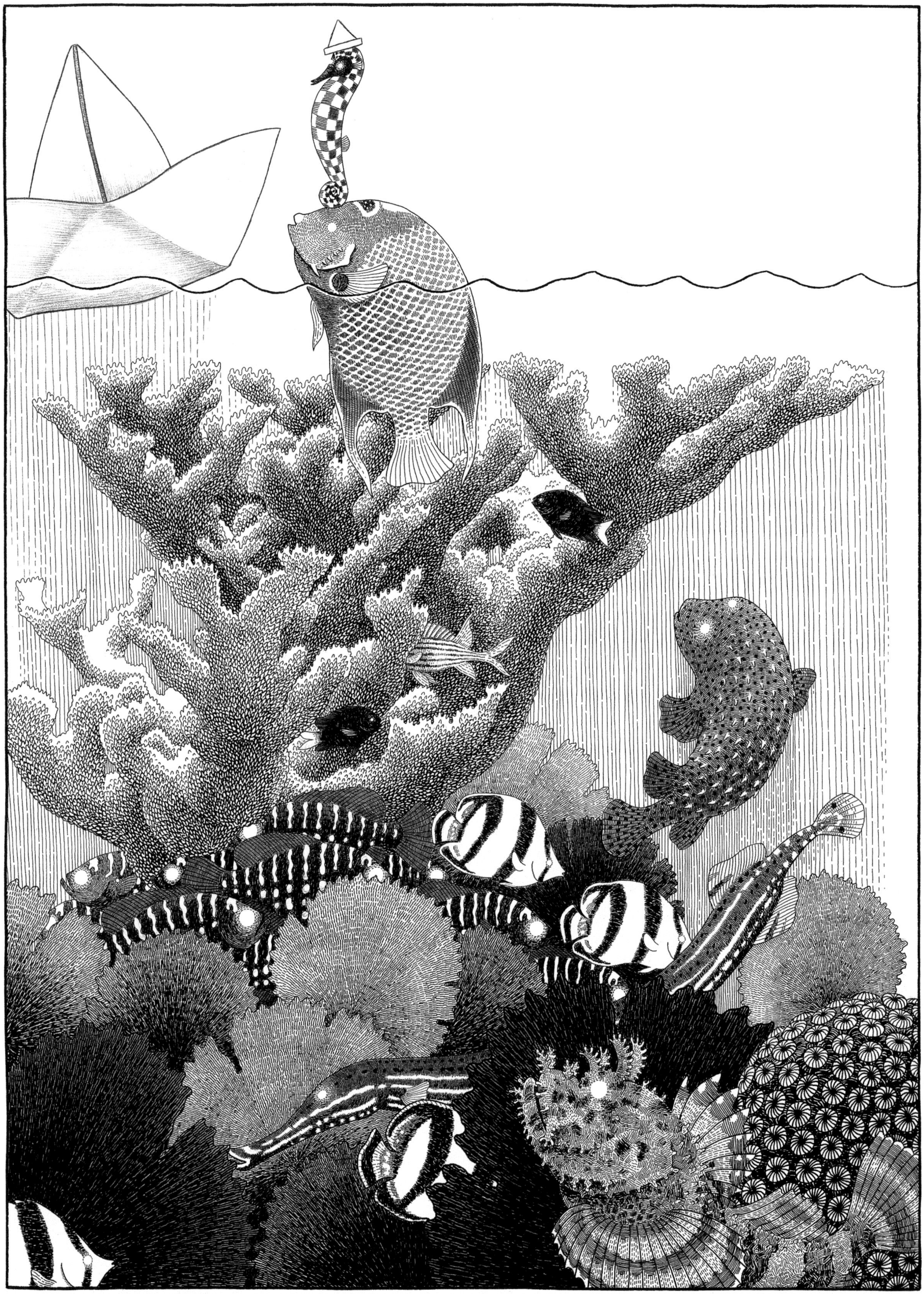

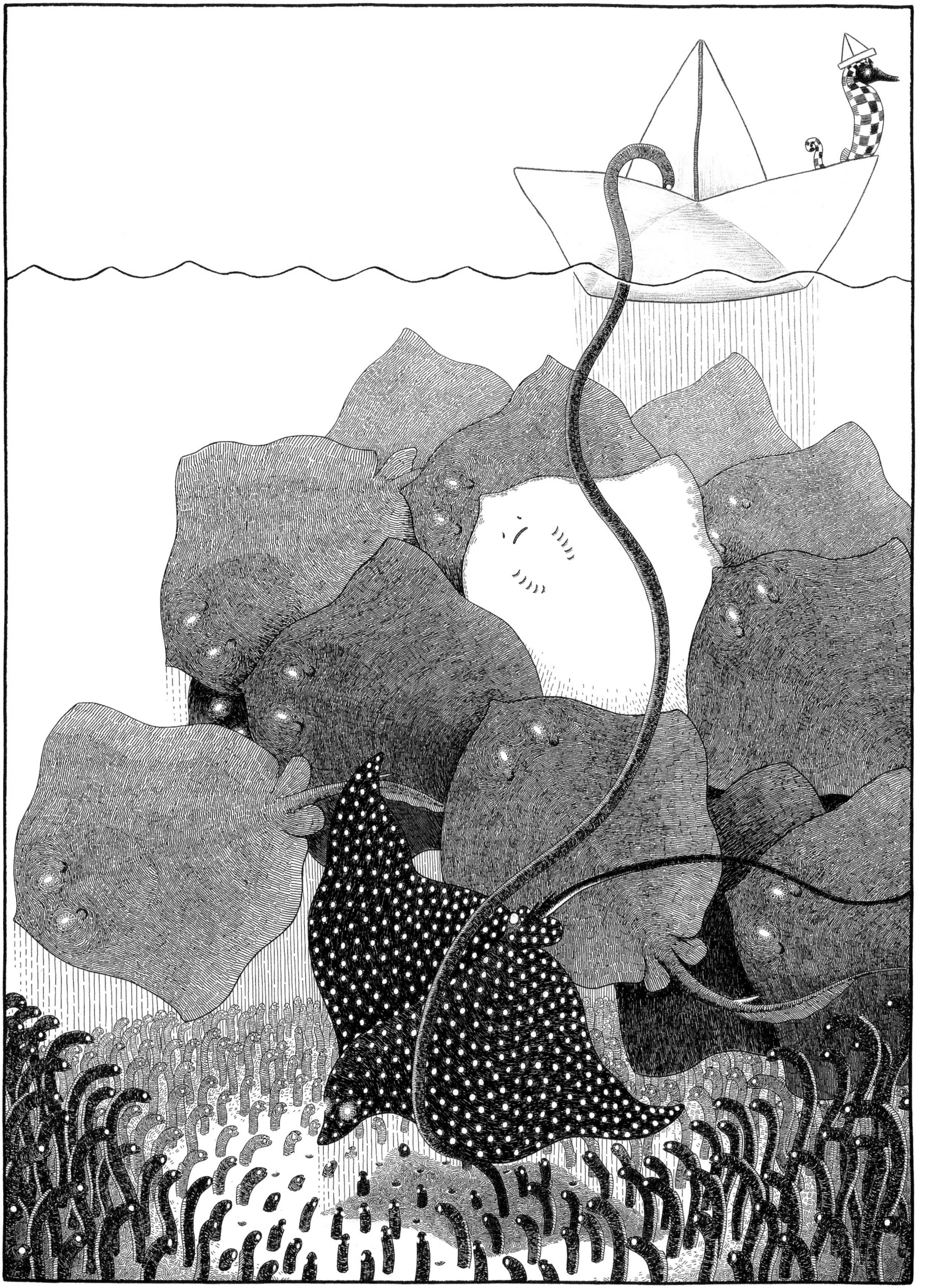

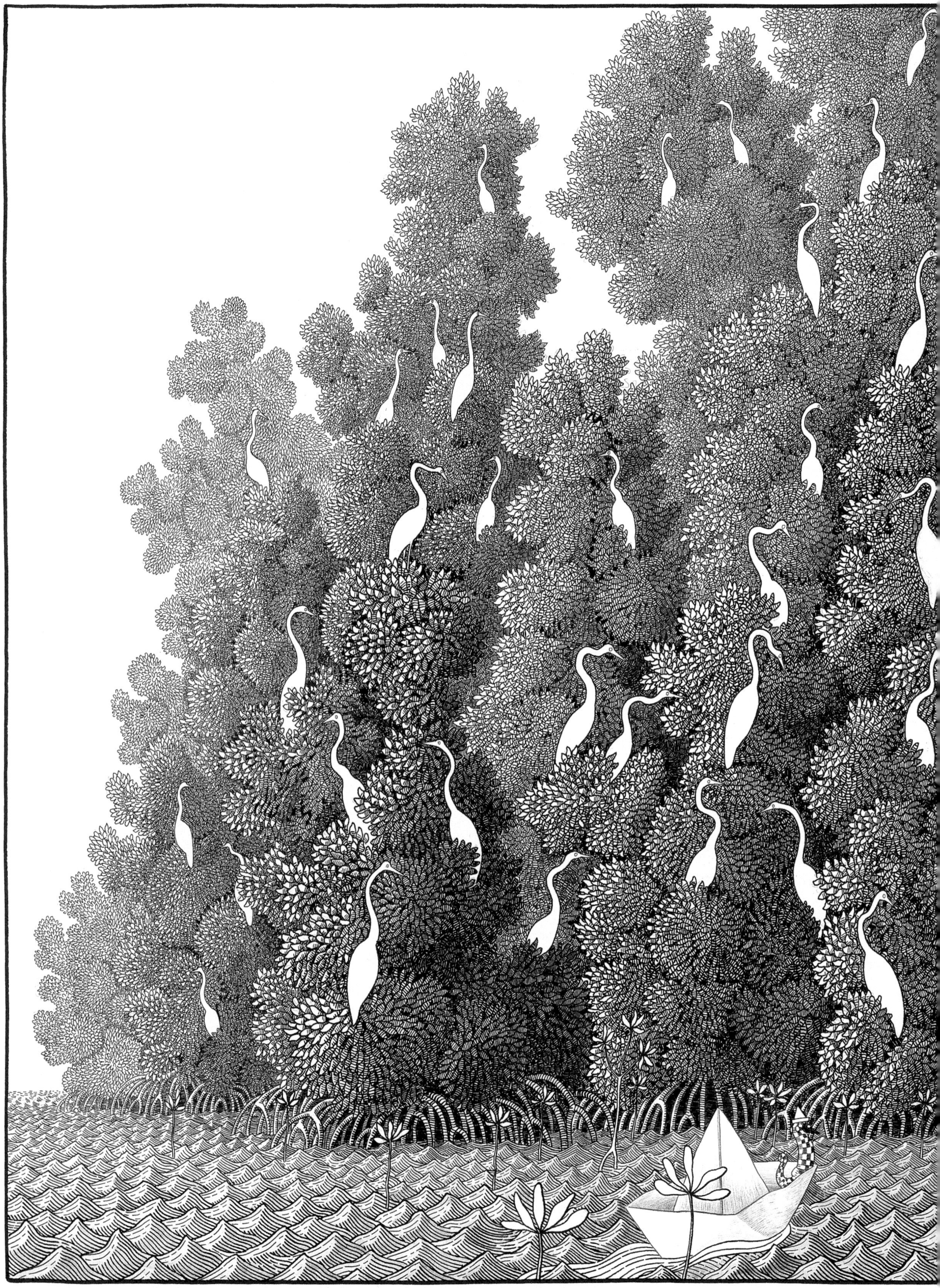

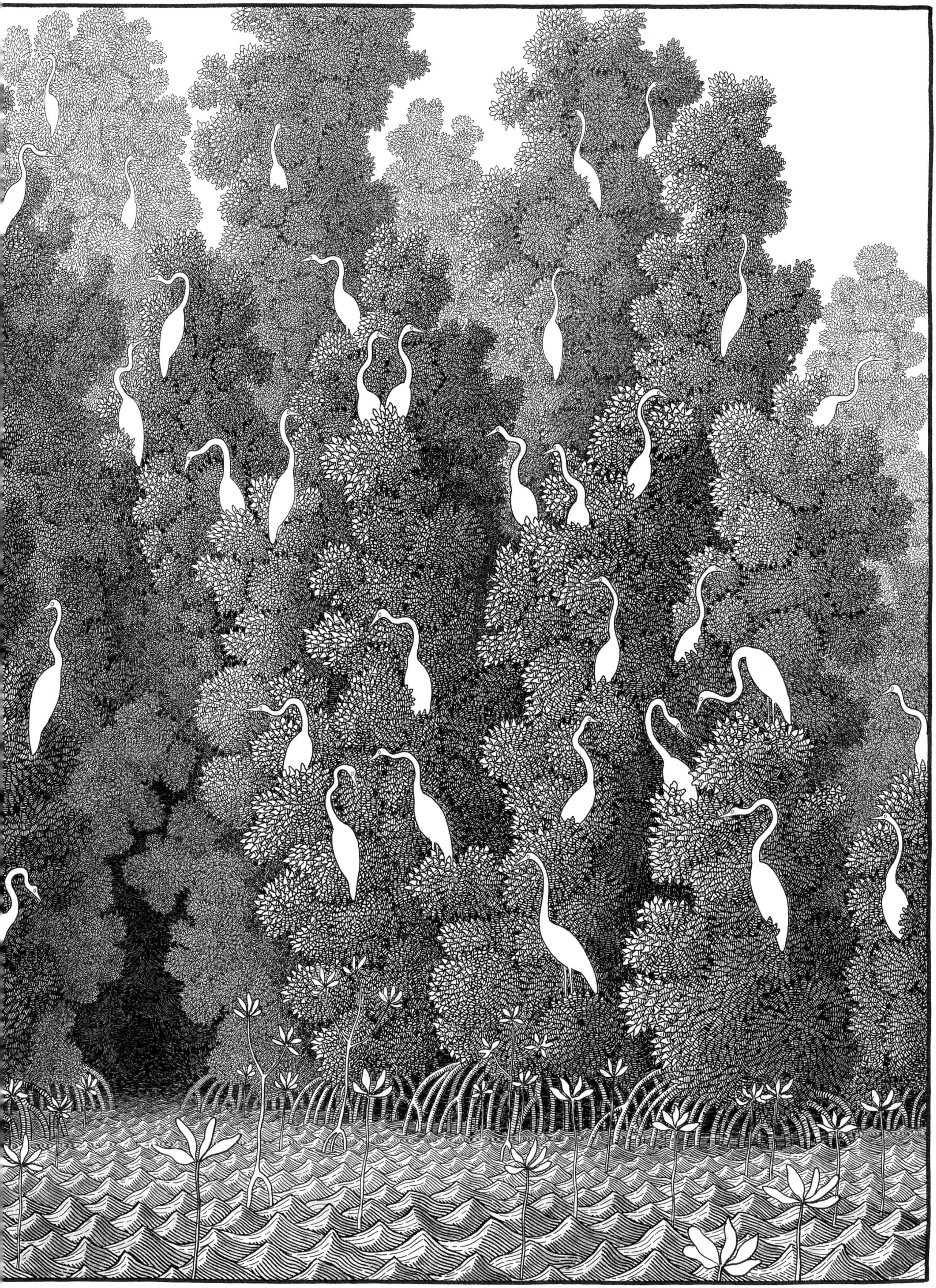

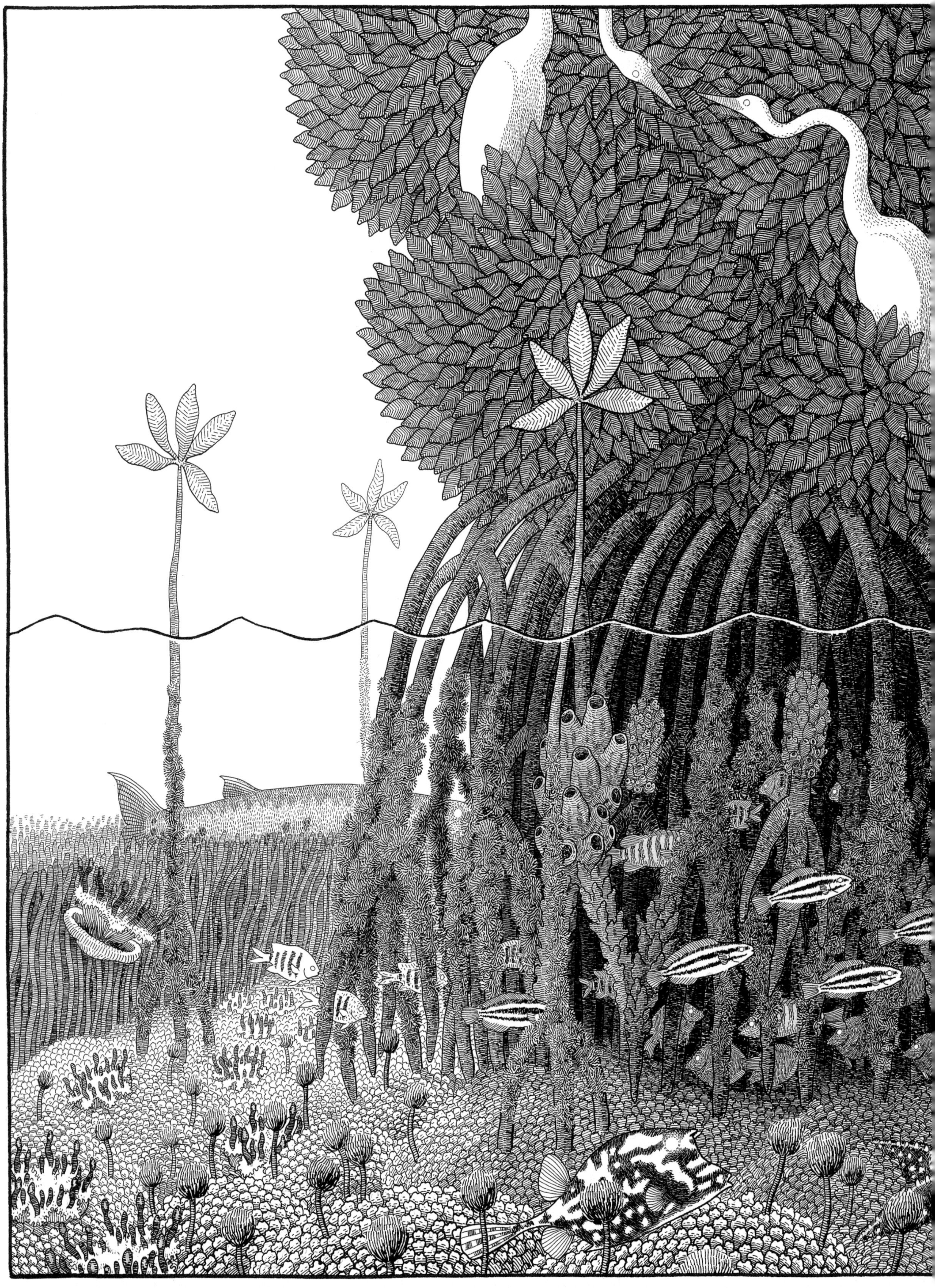

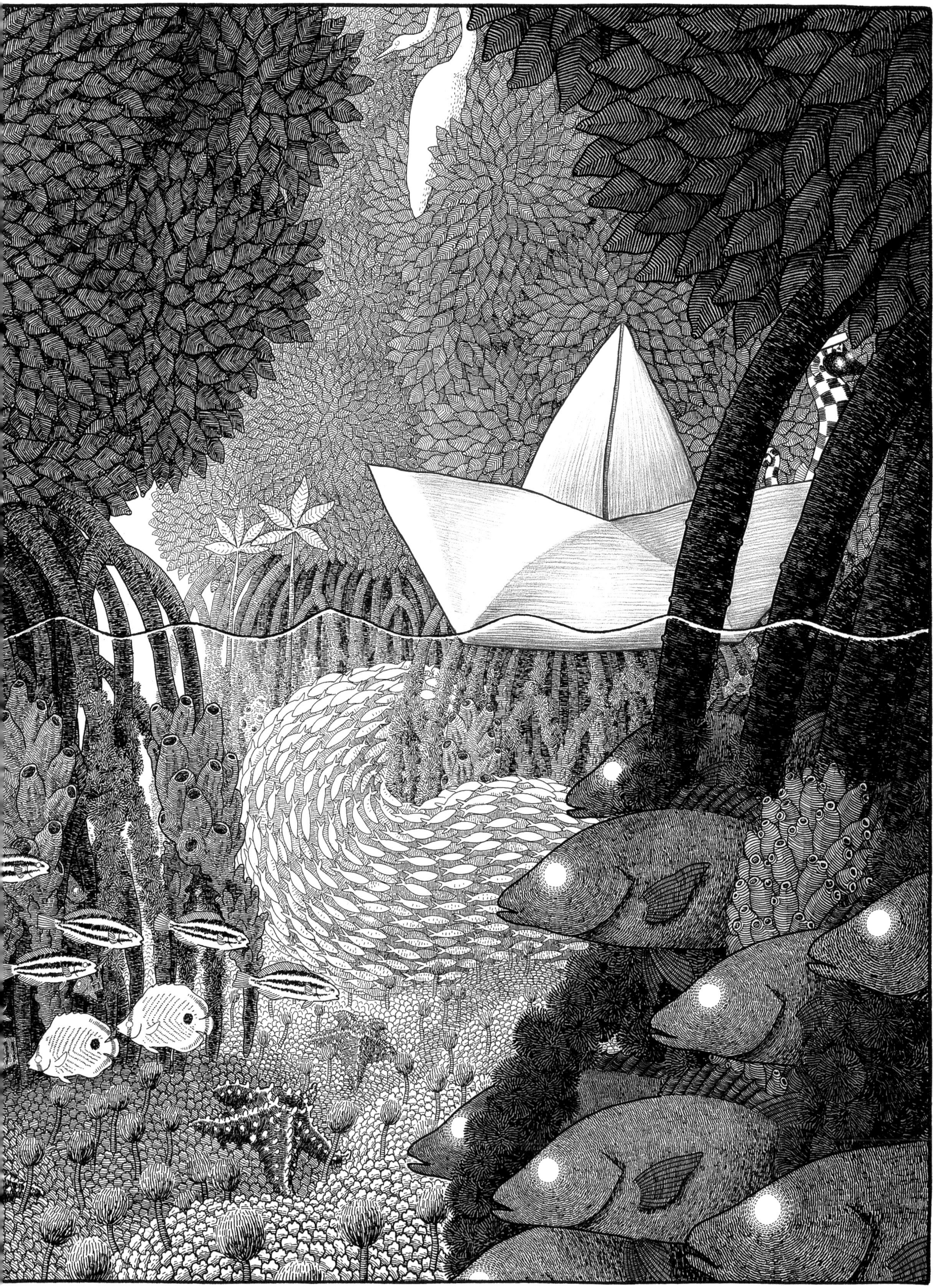

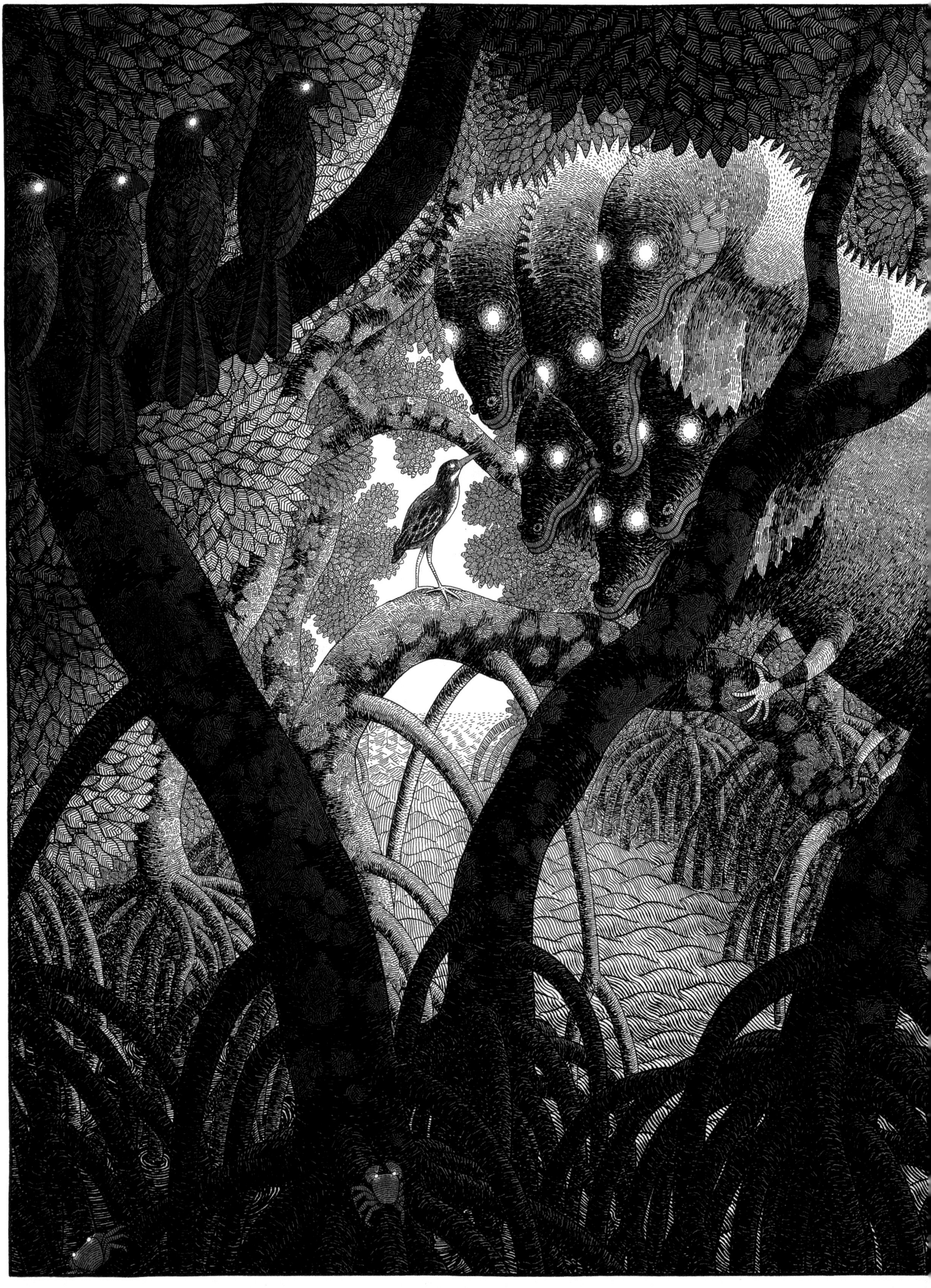

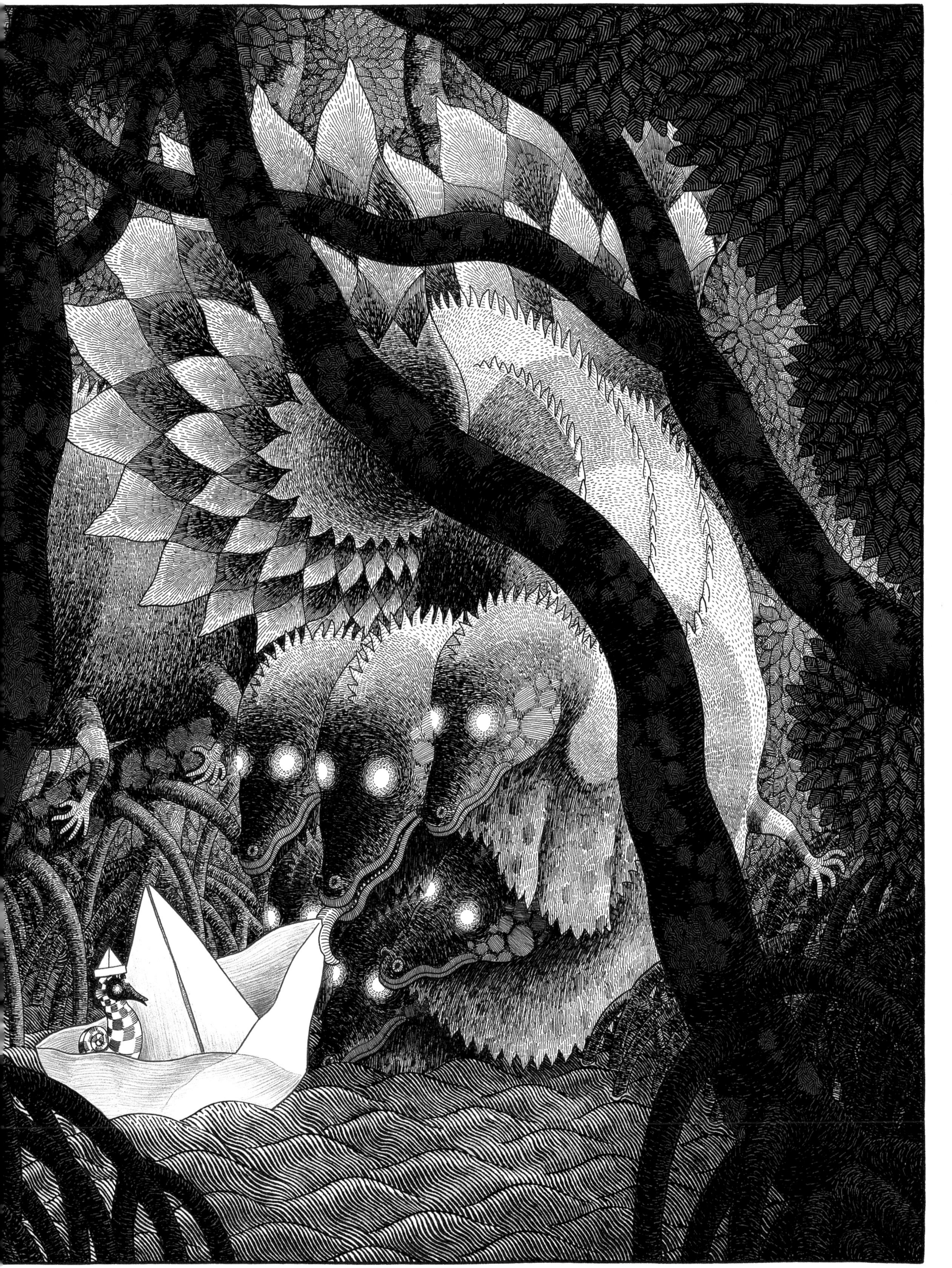

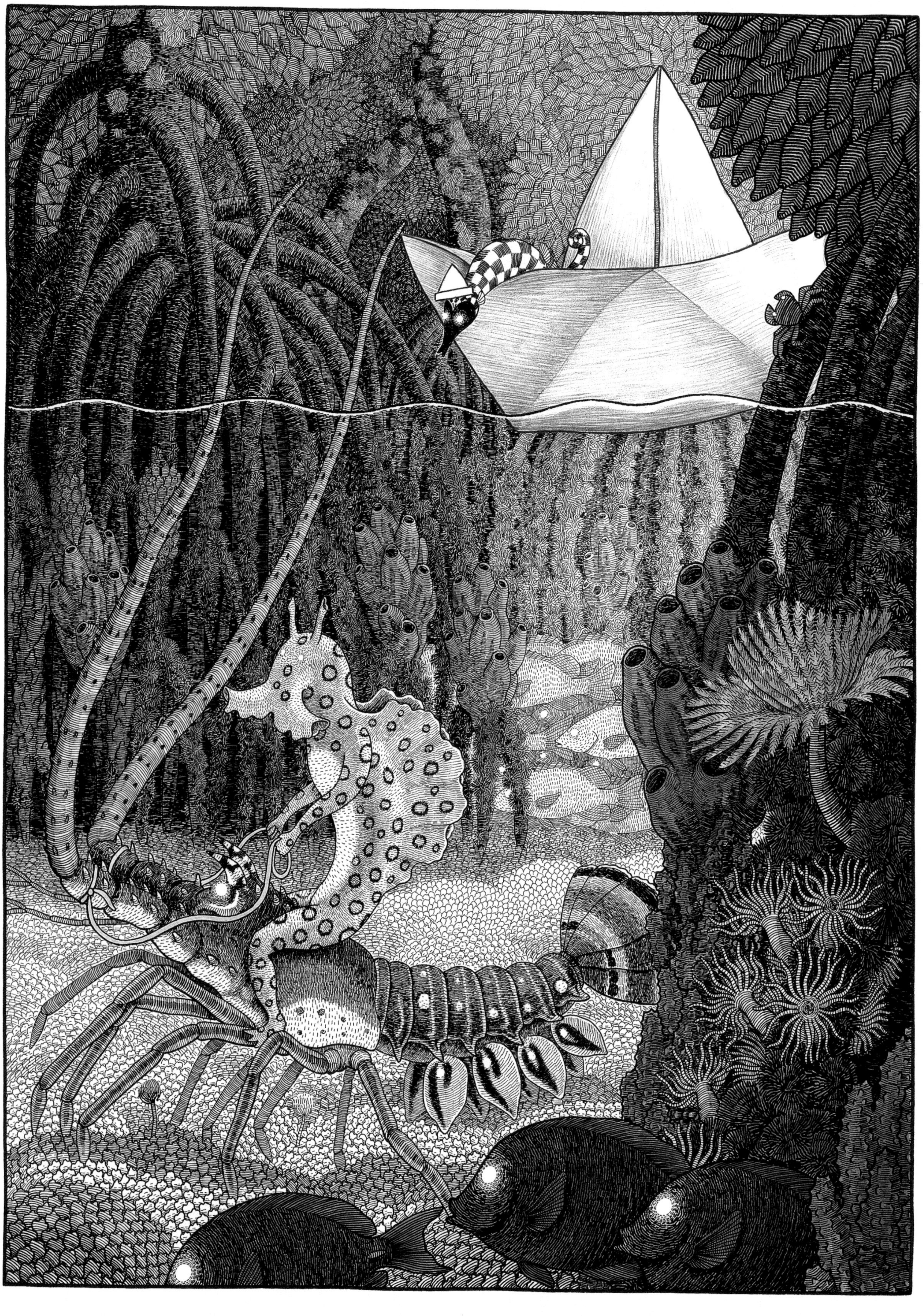

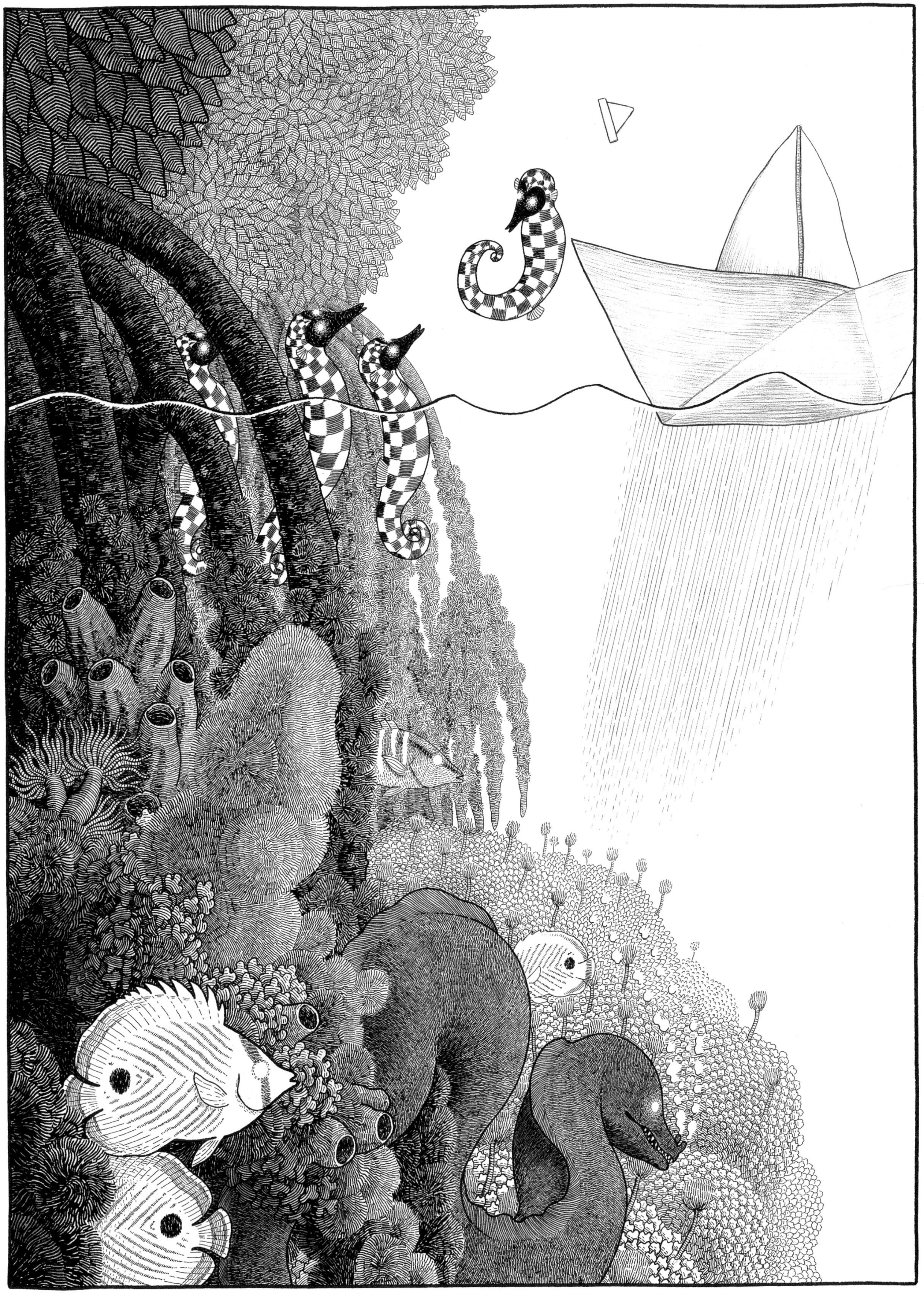

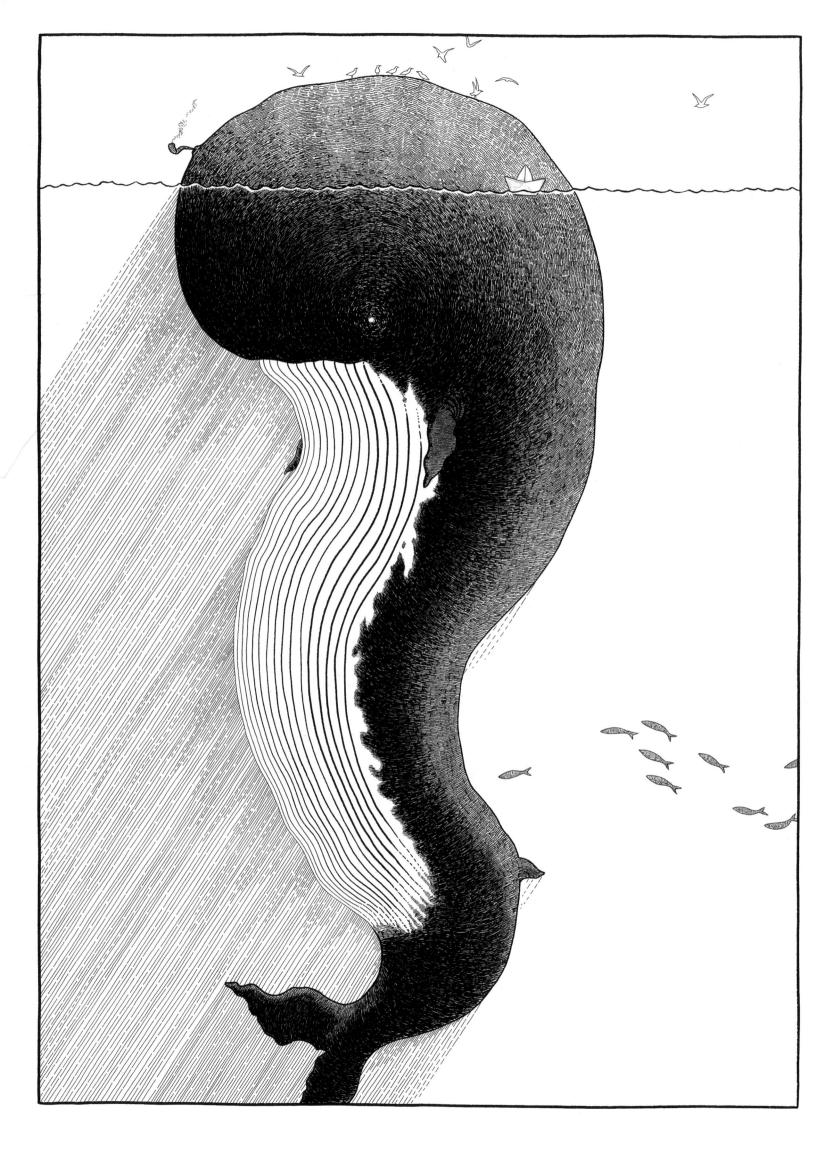

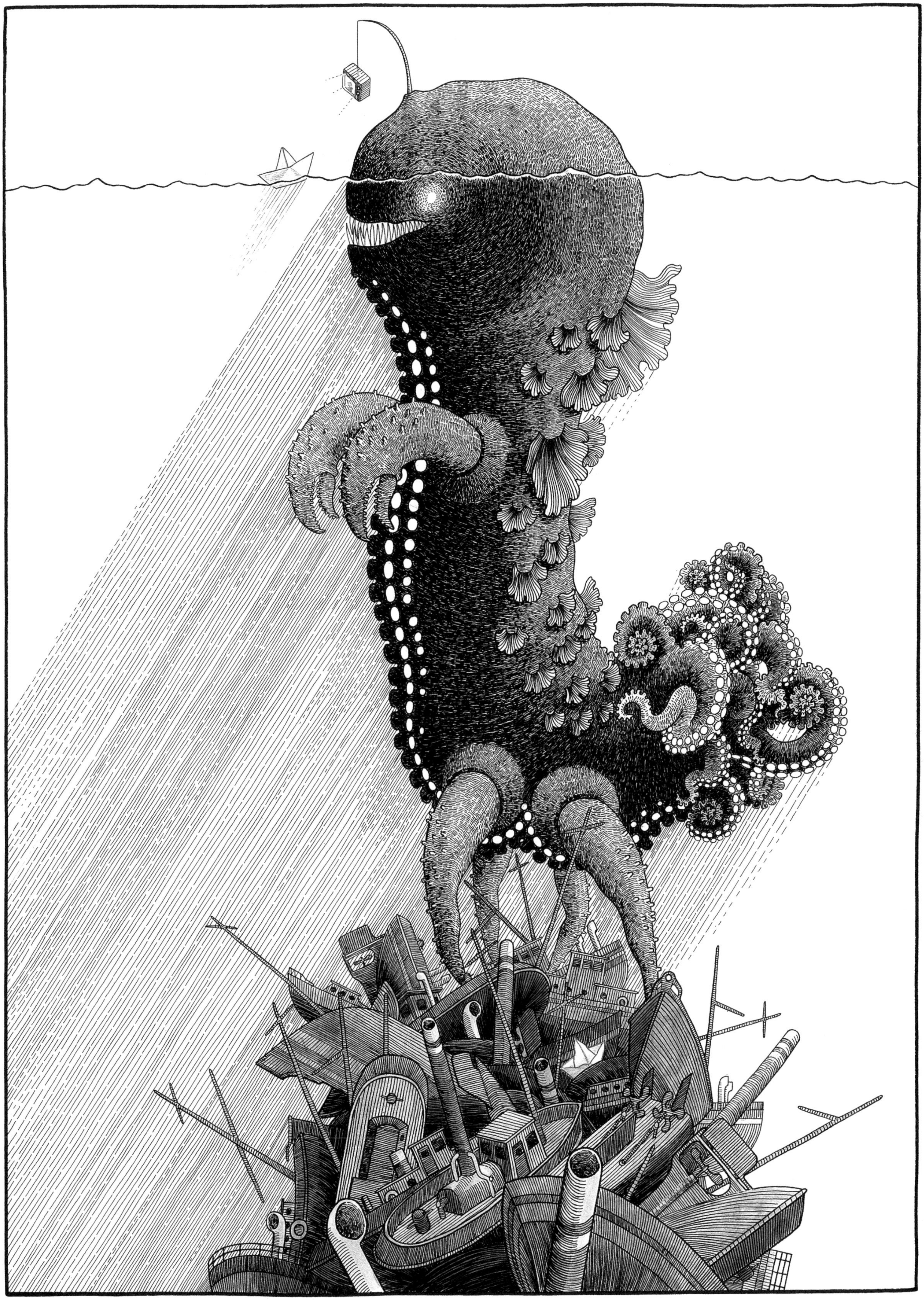

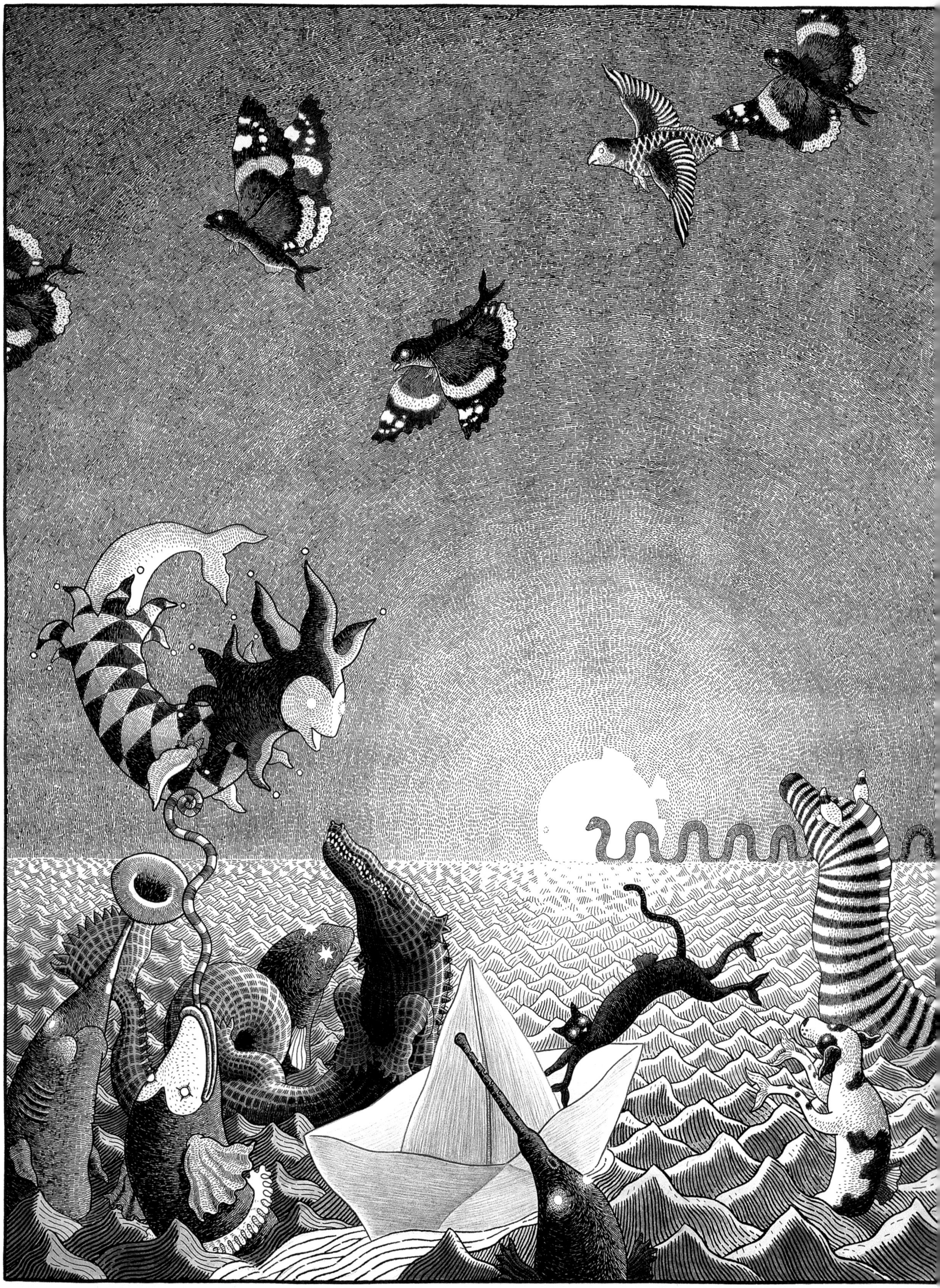

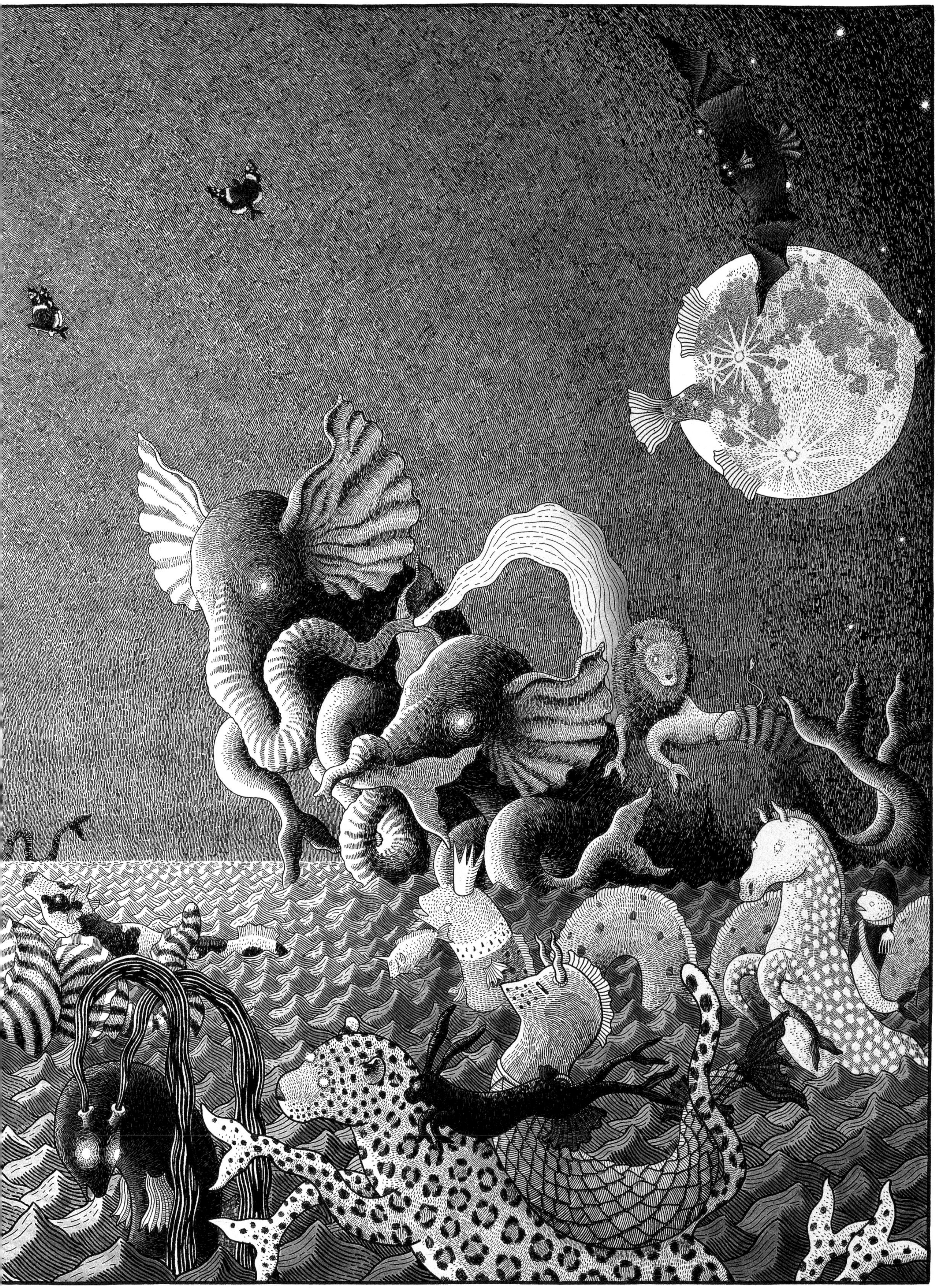

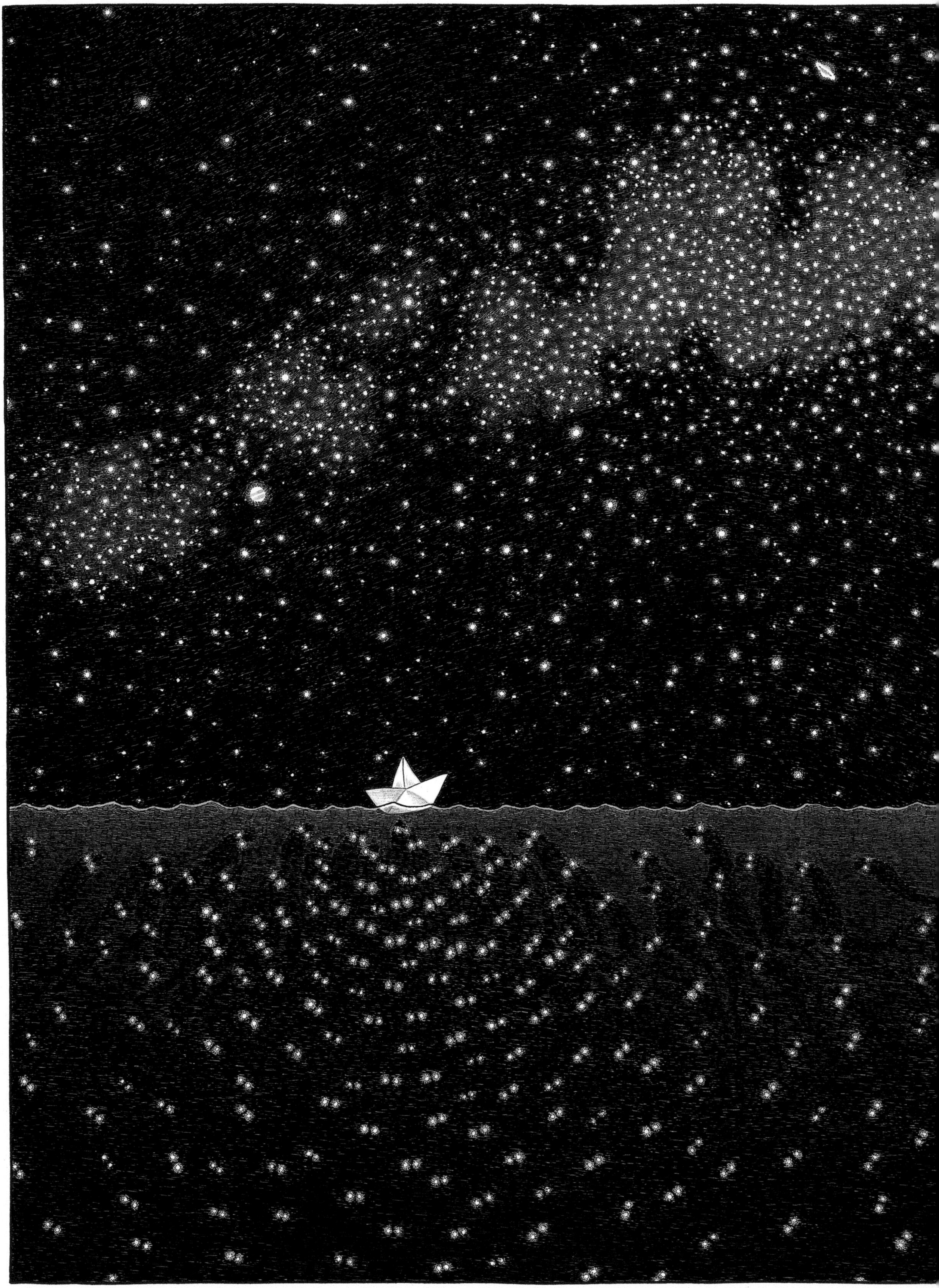

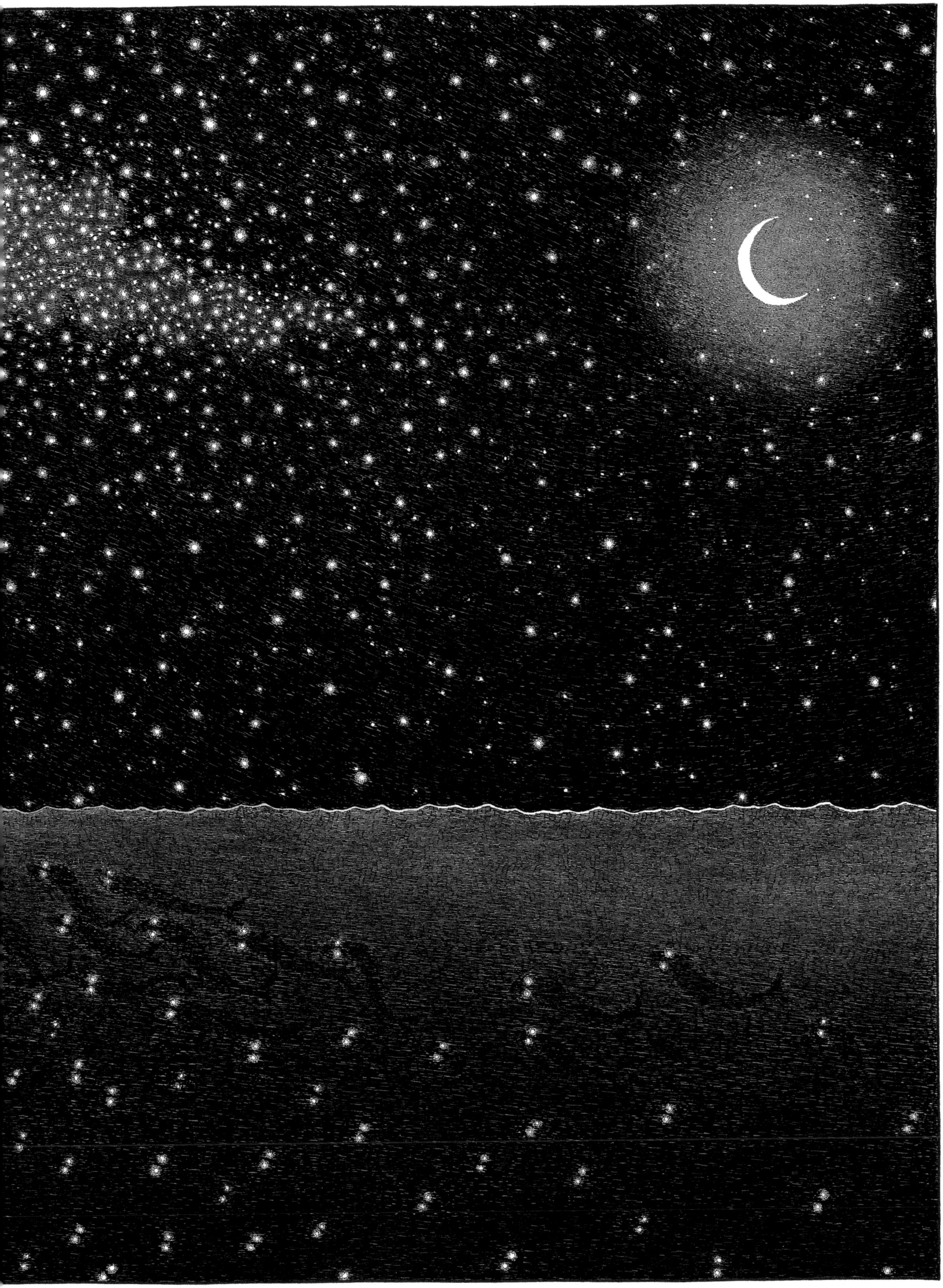

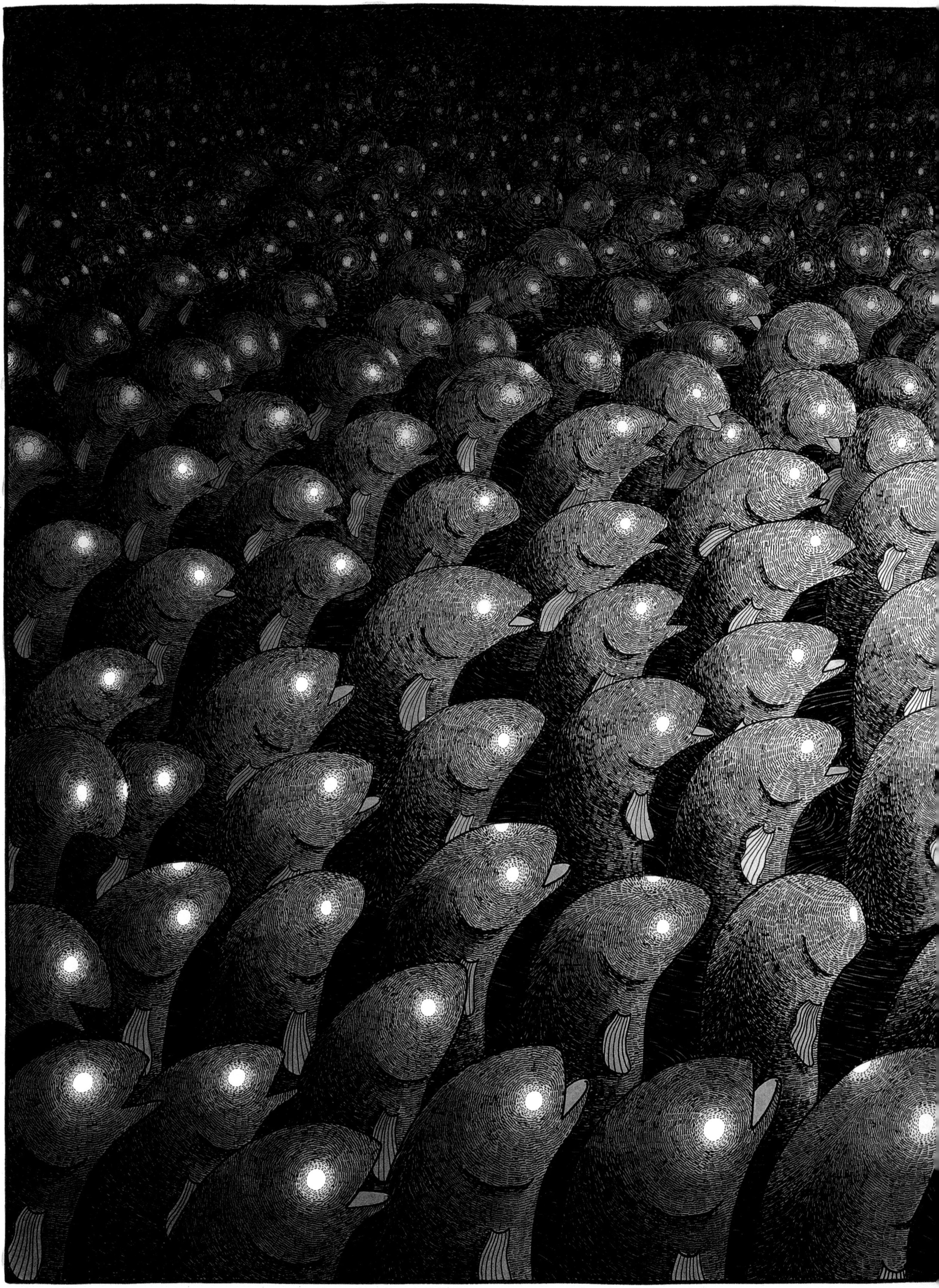

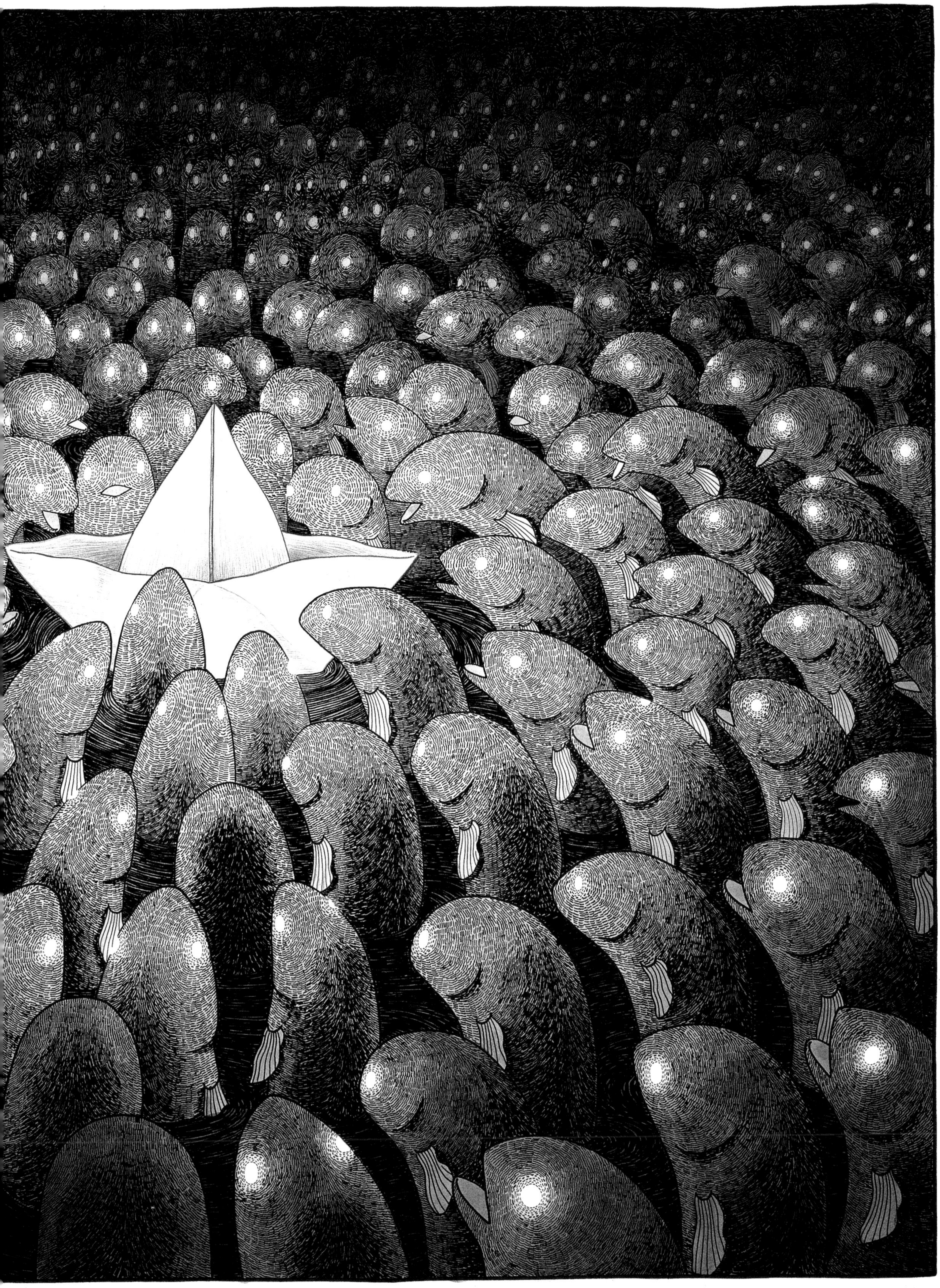

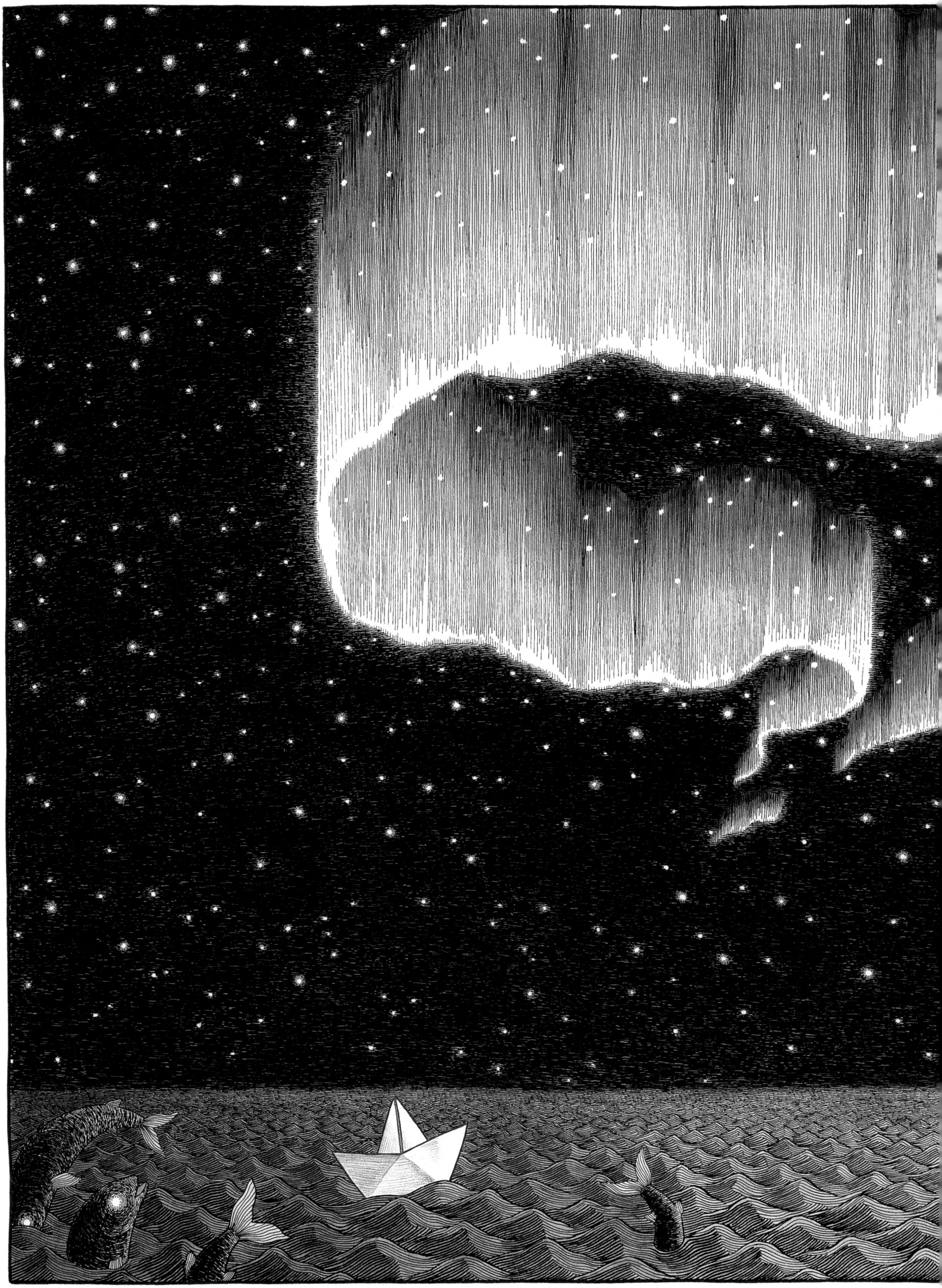

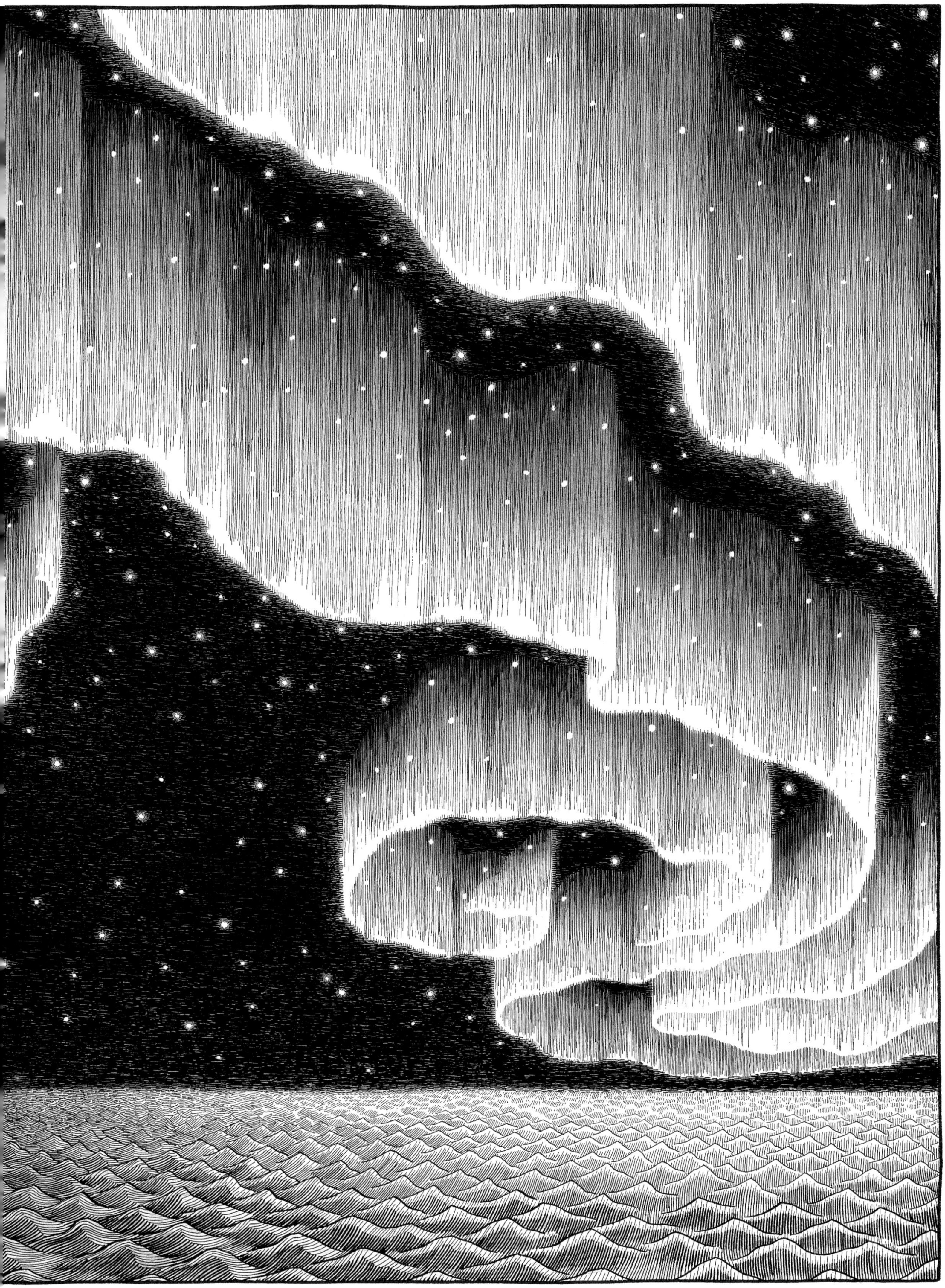

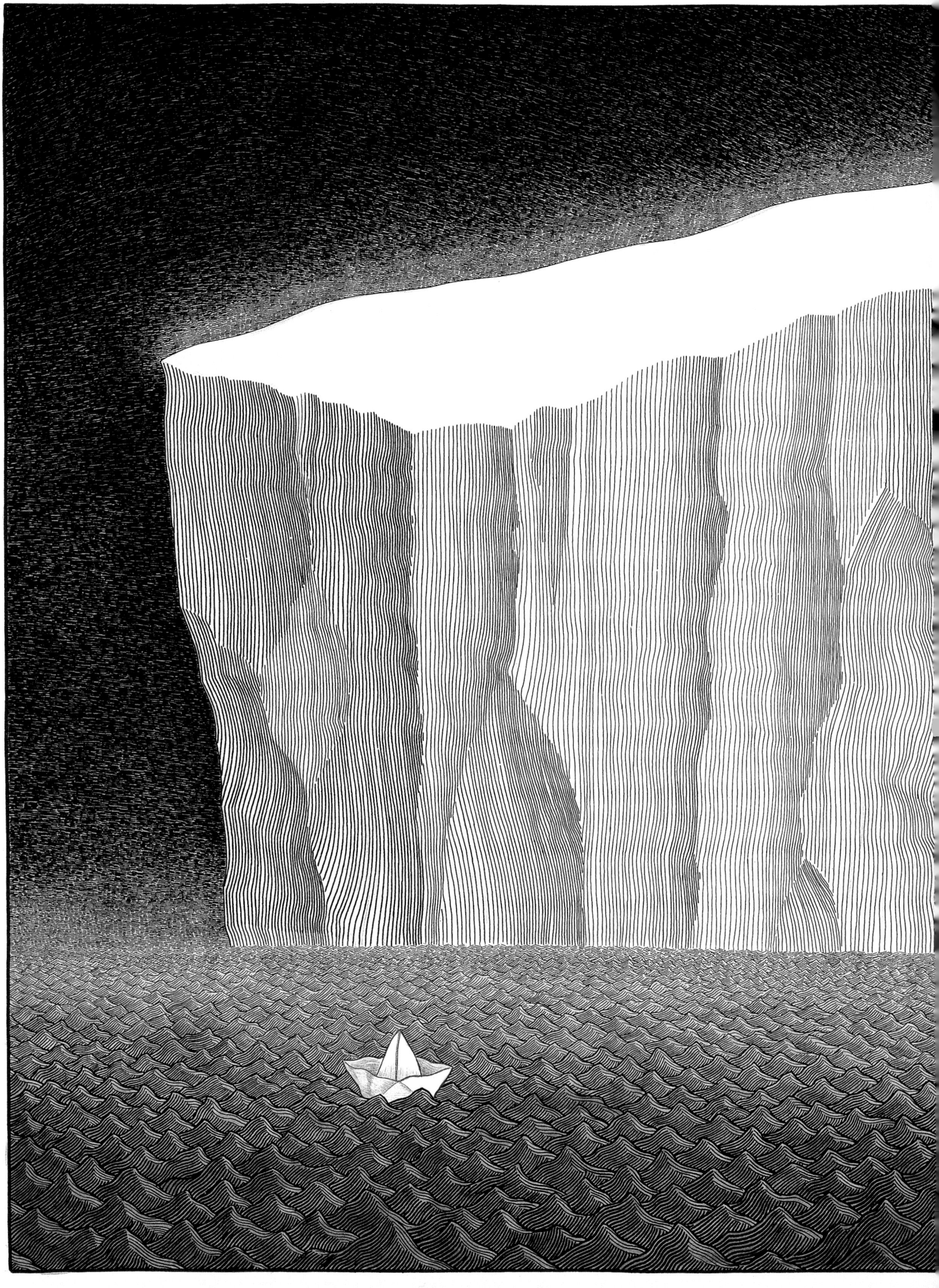

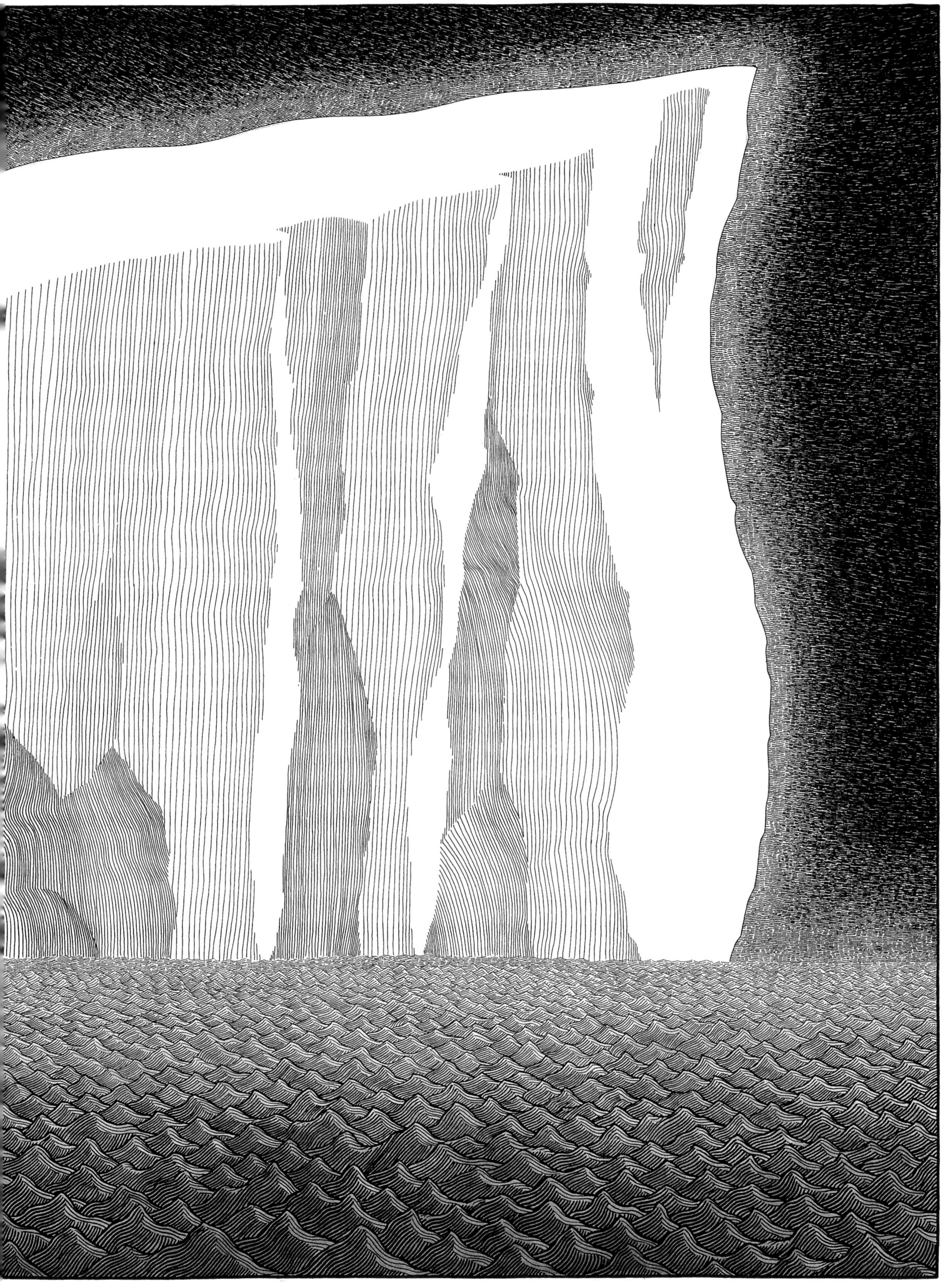

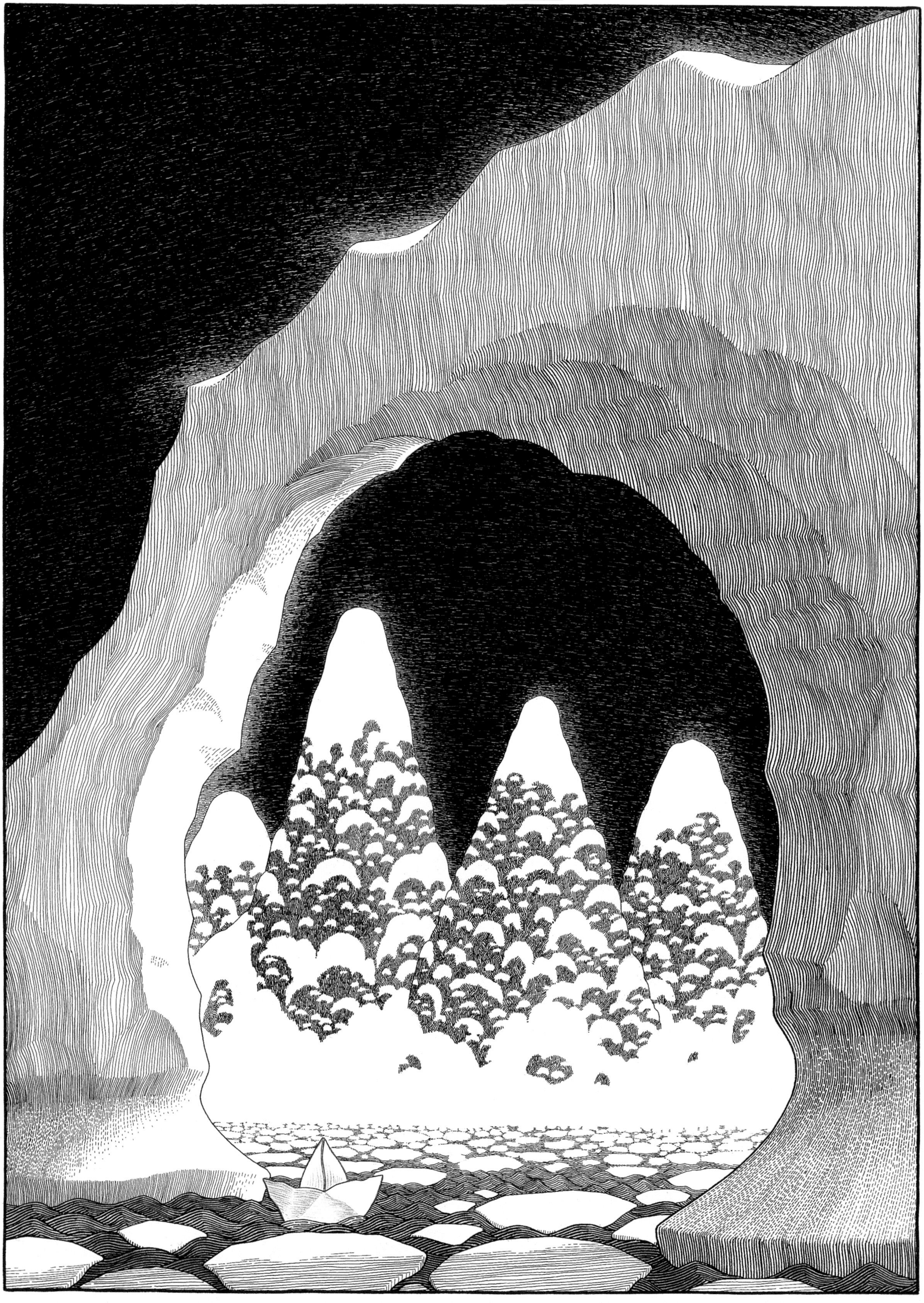

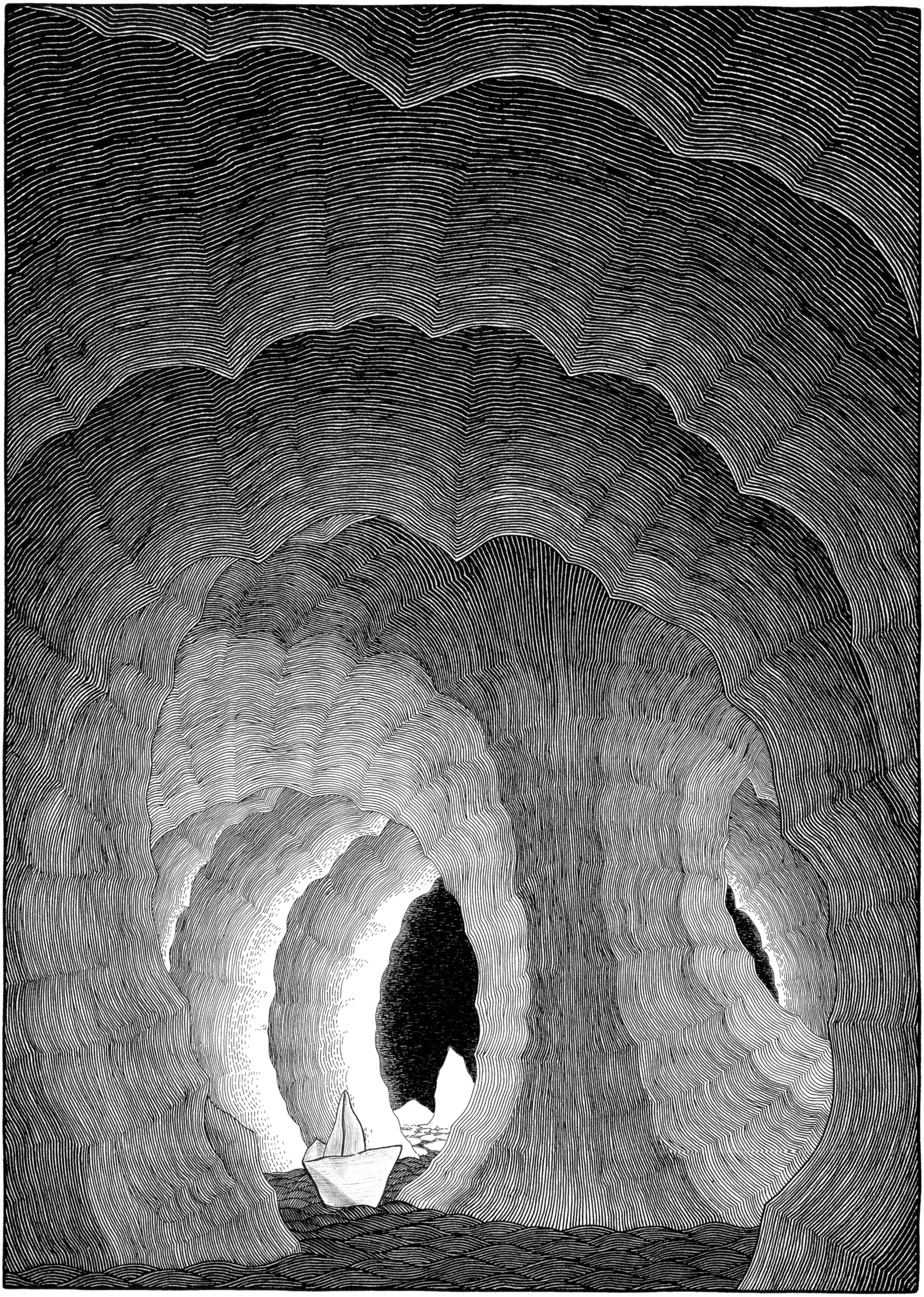

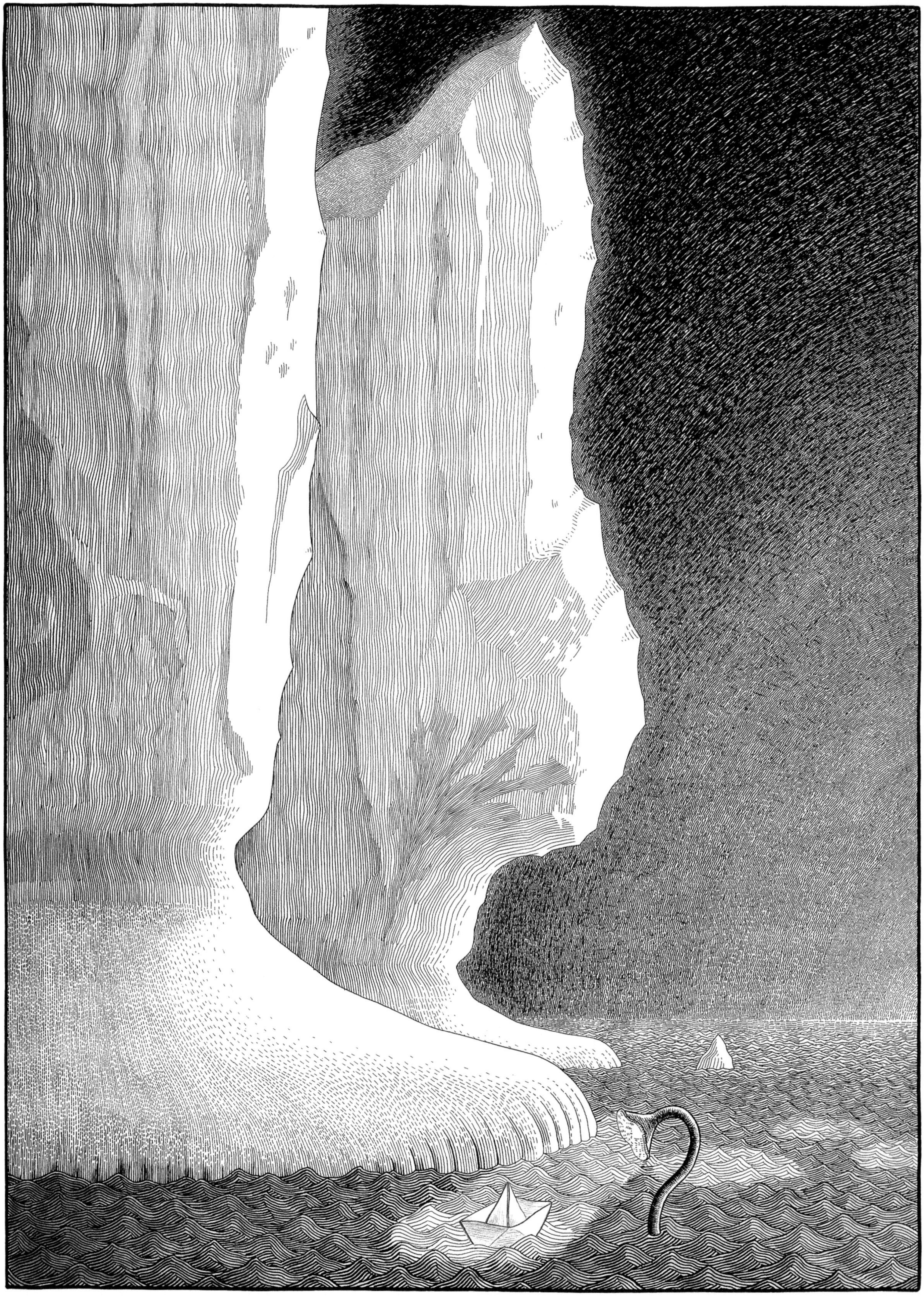

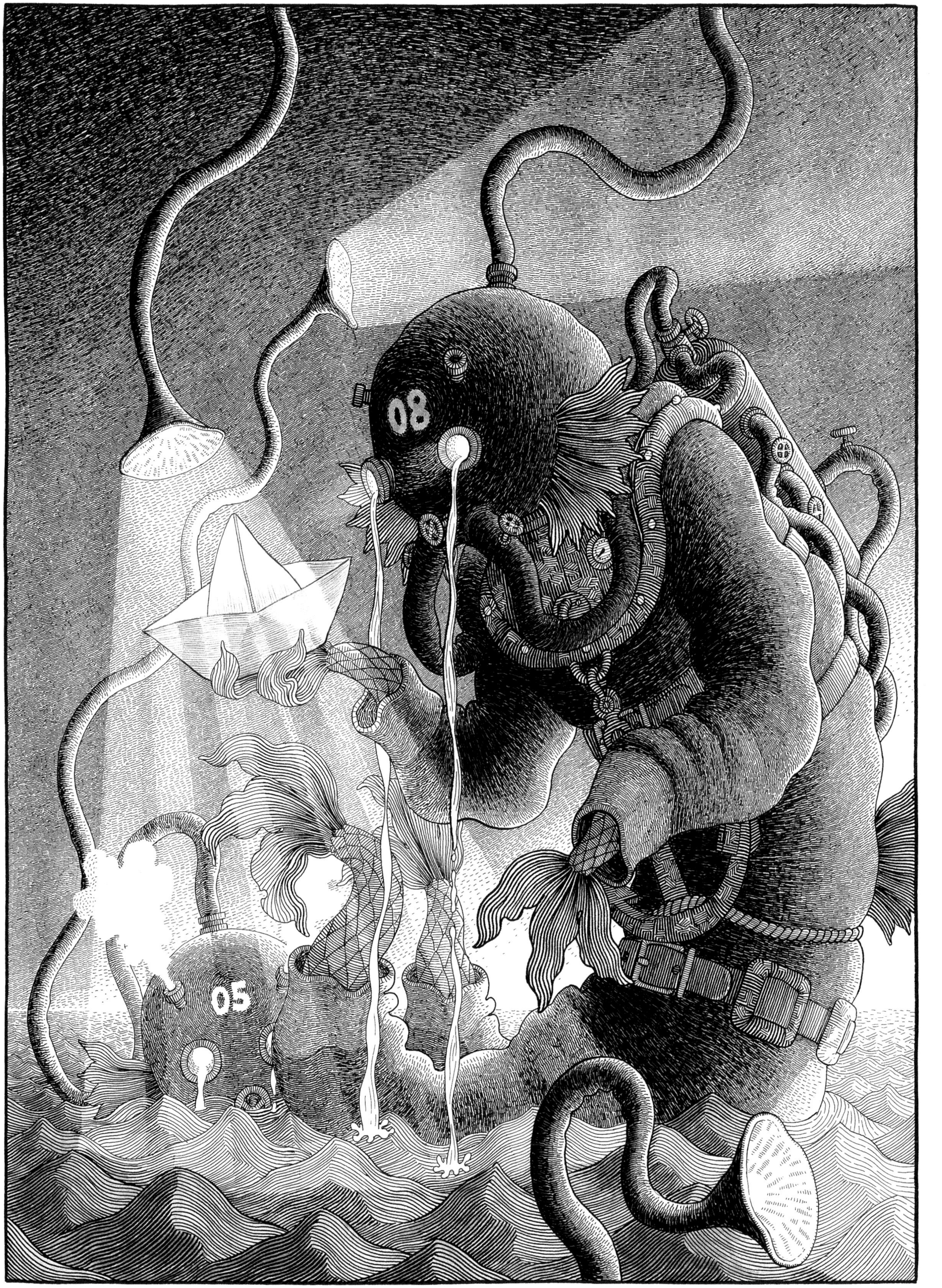
08
05

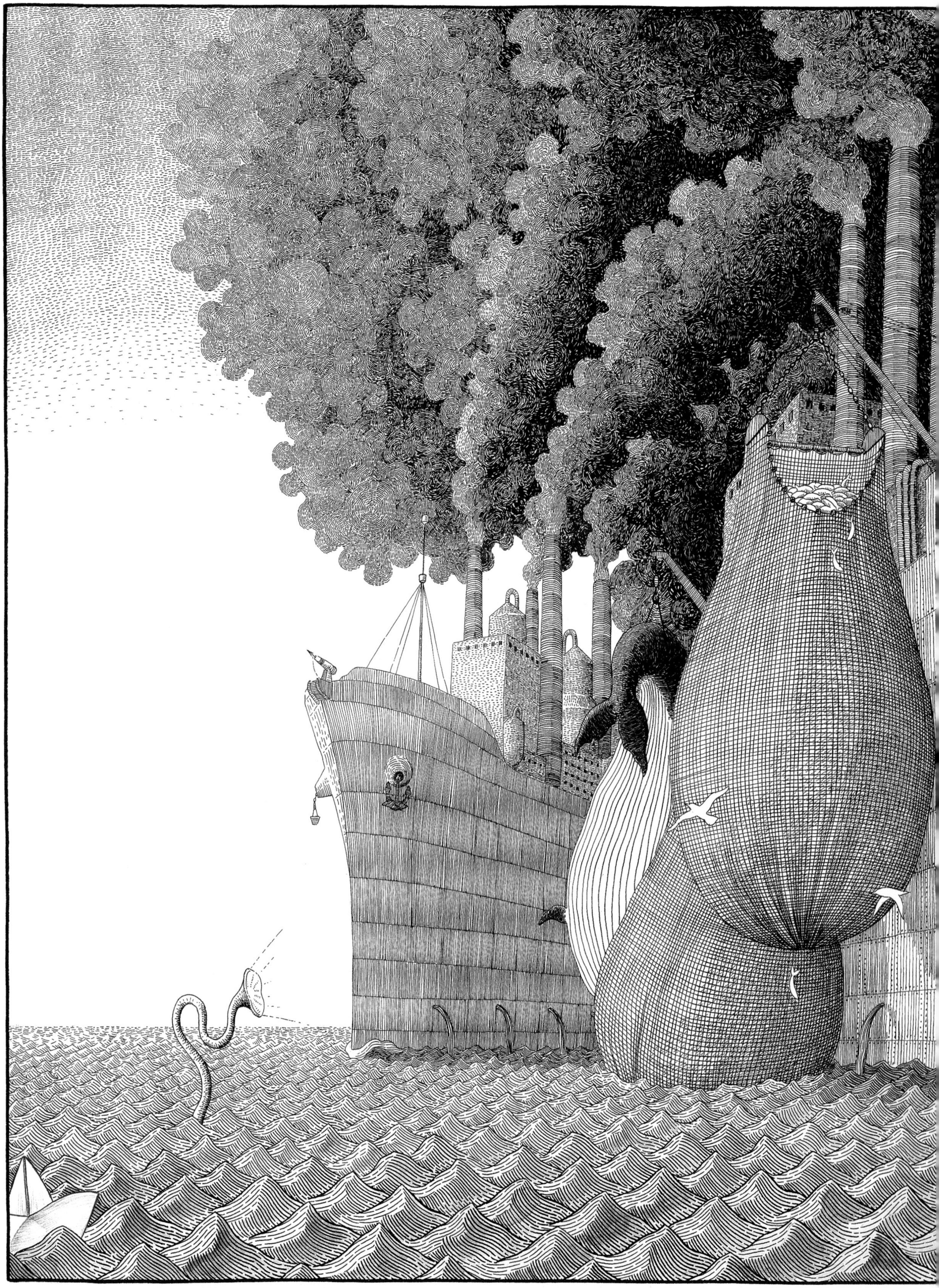

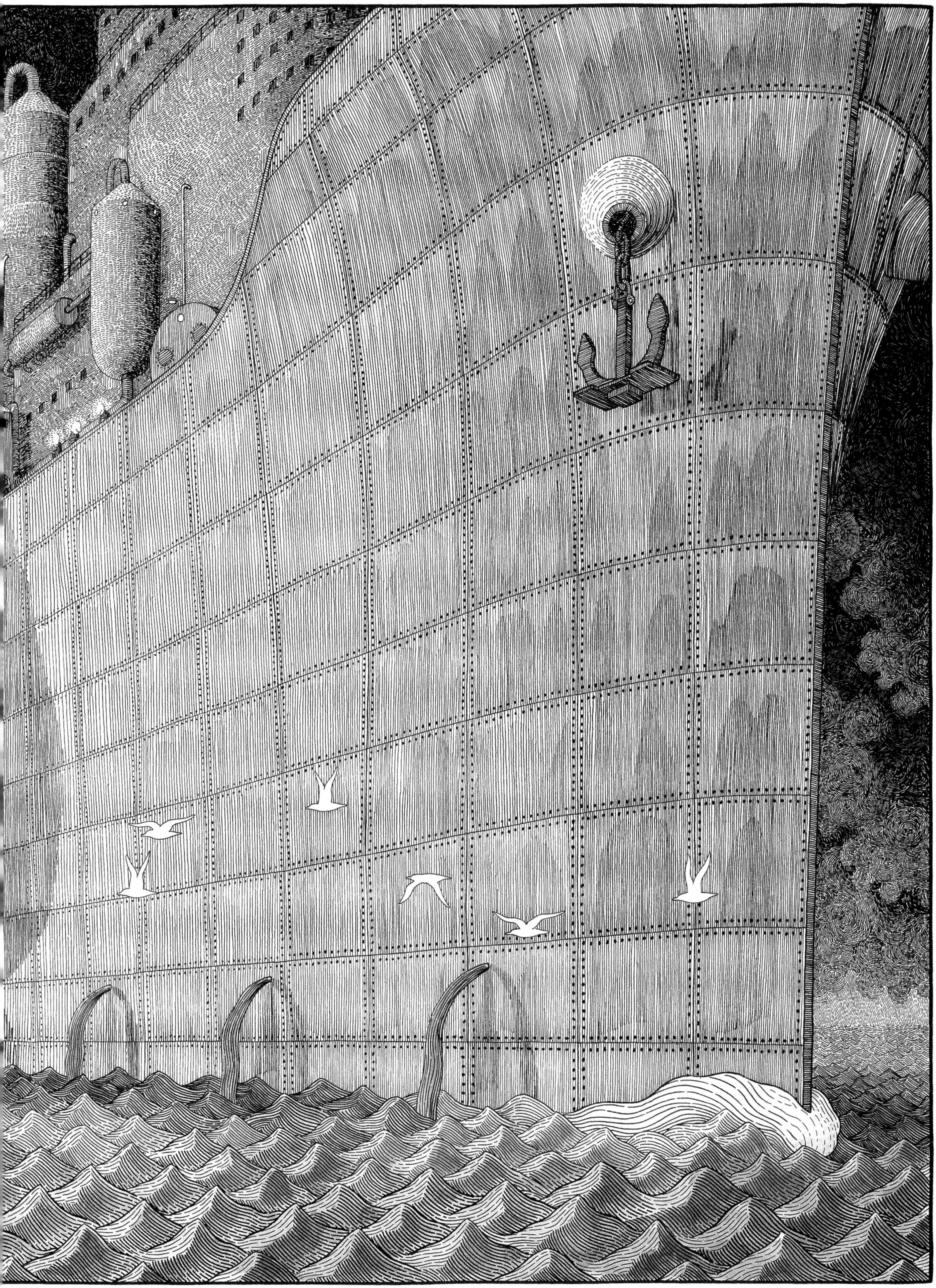

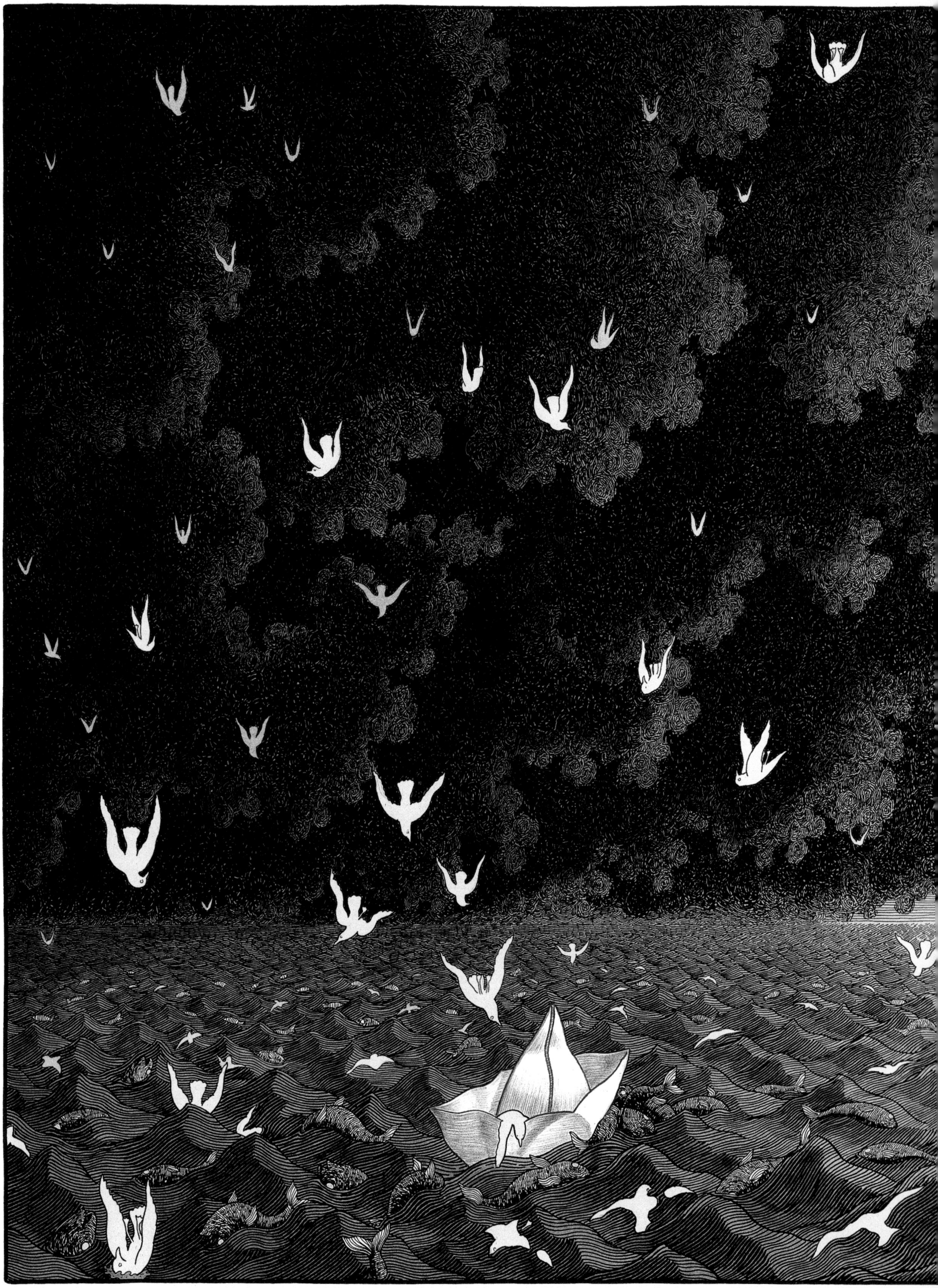

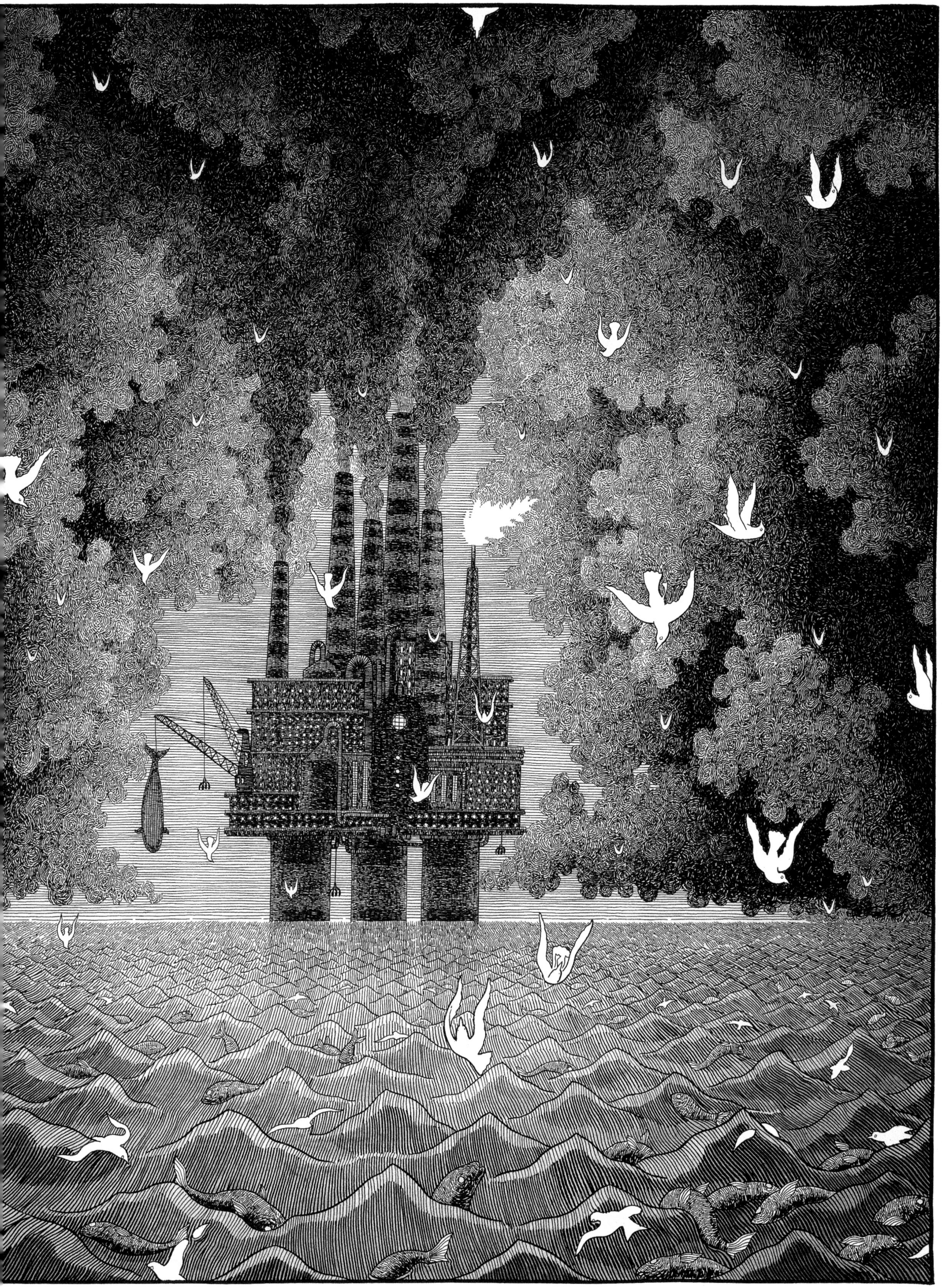

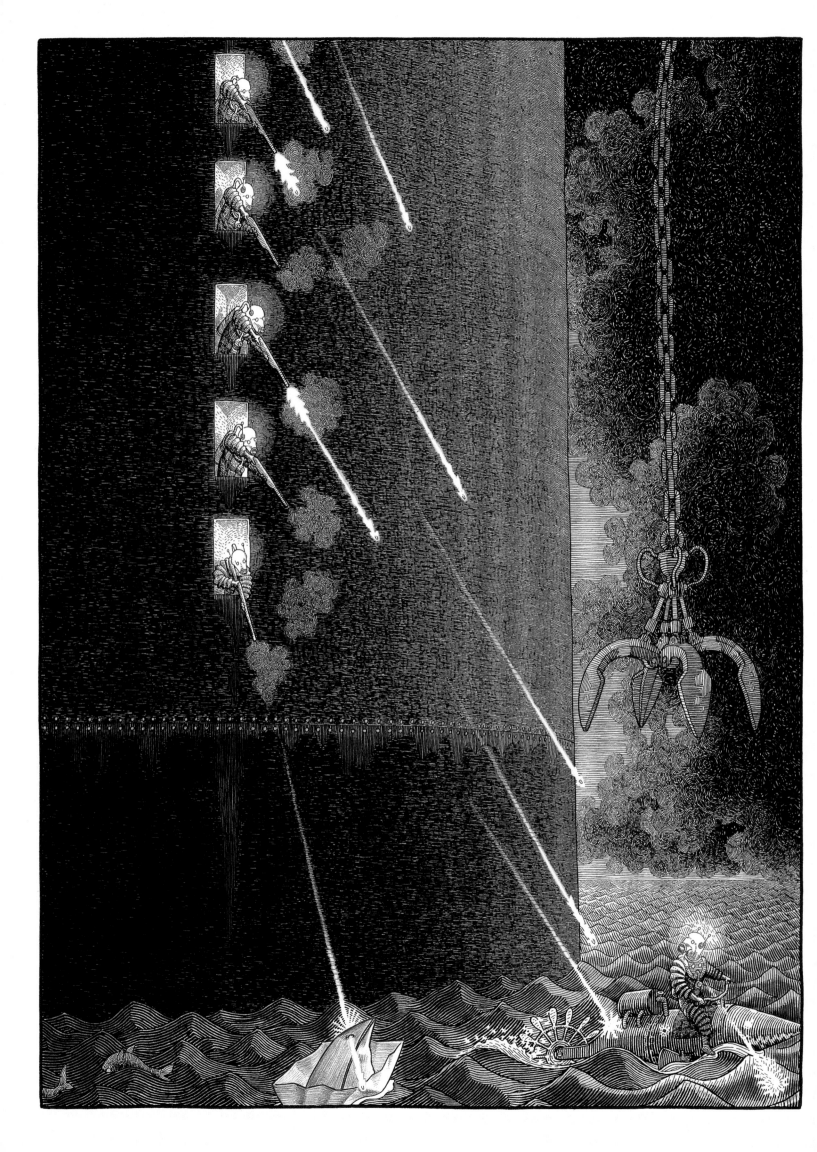

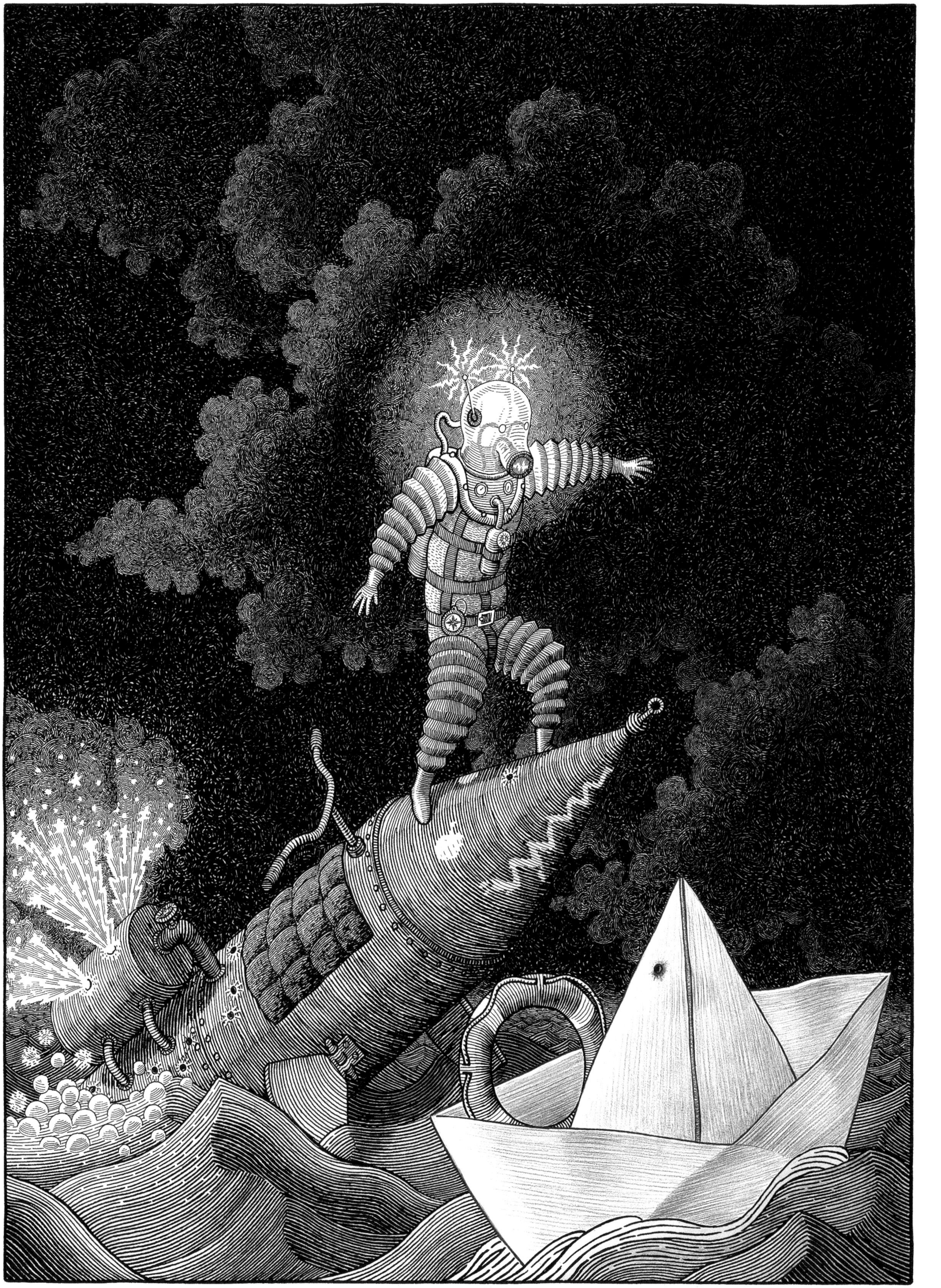

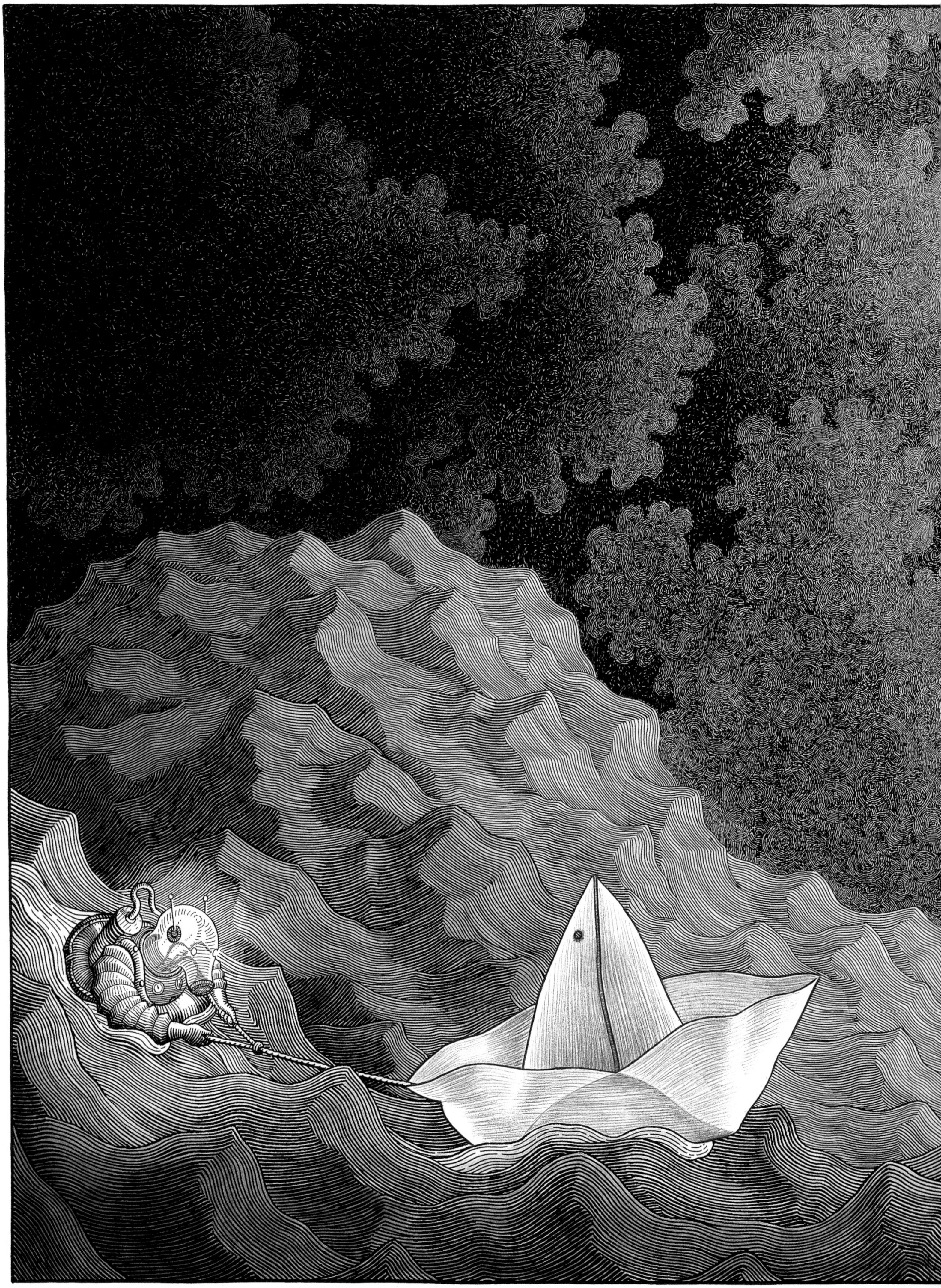

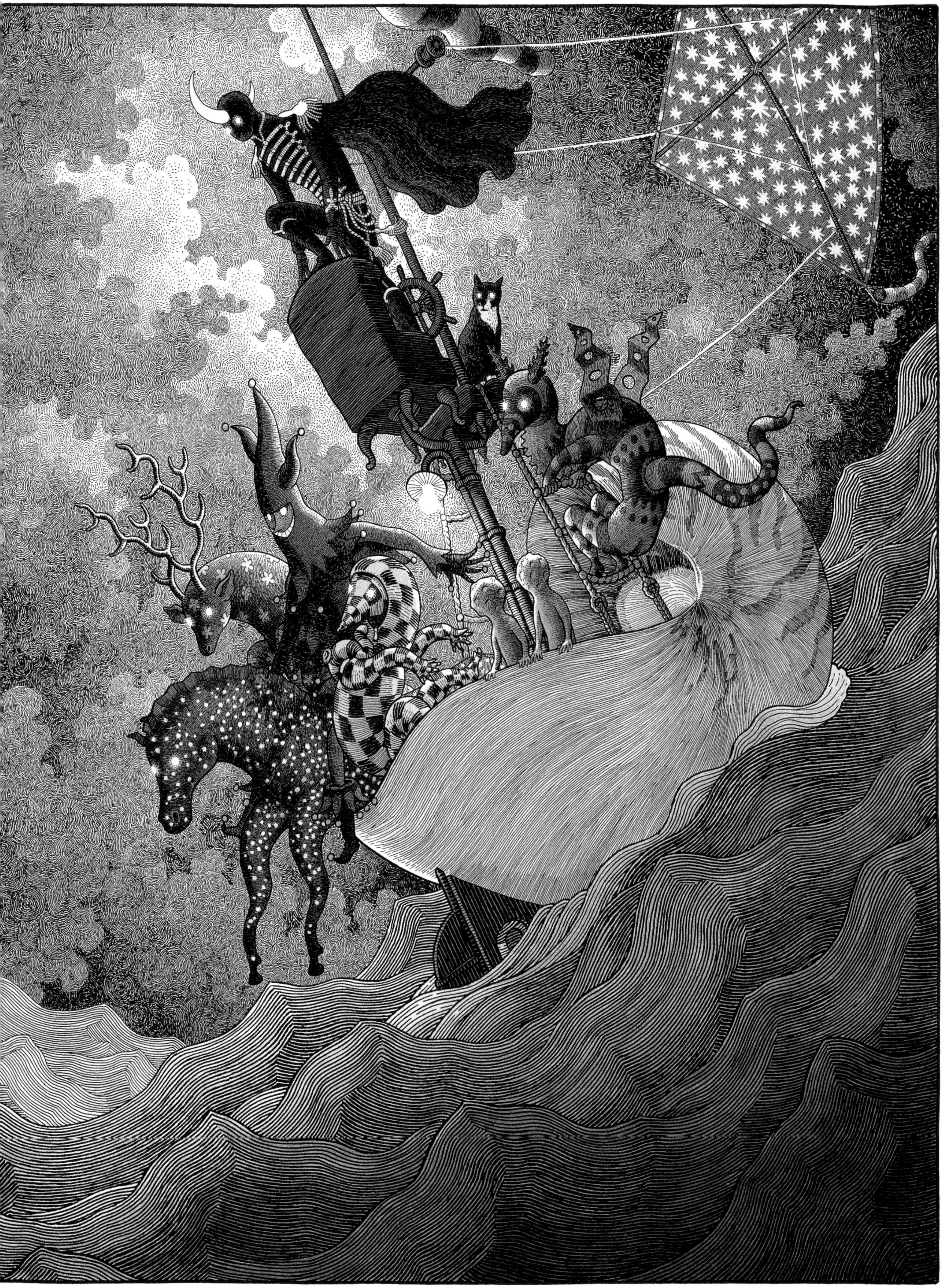

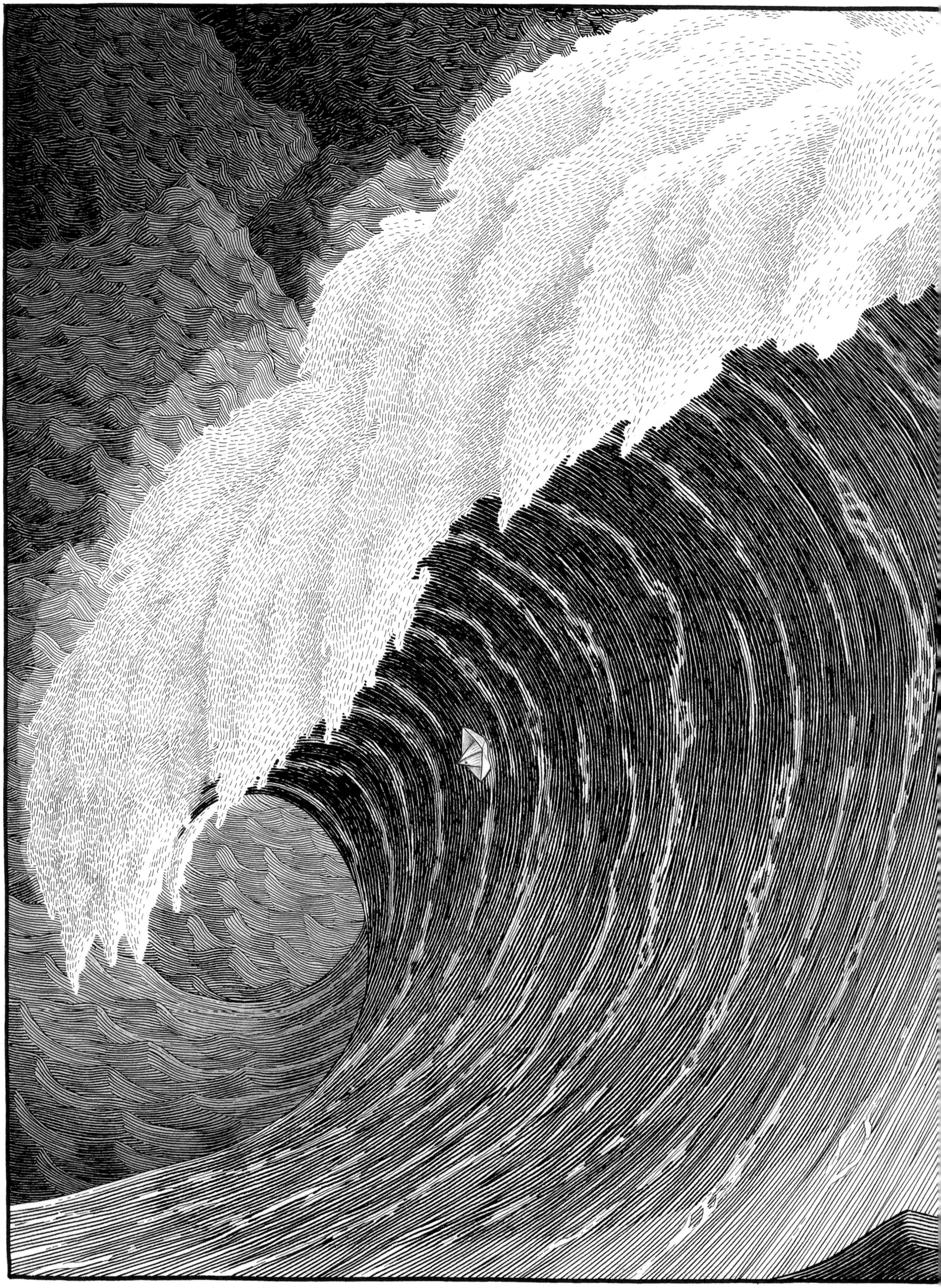

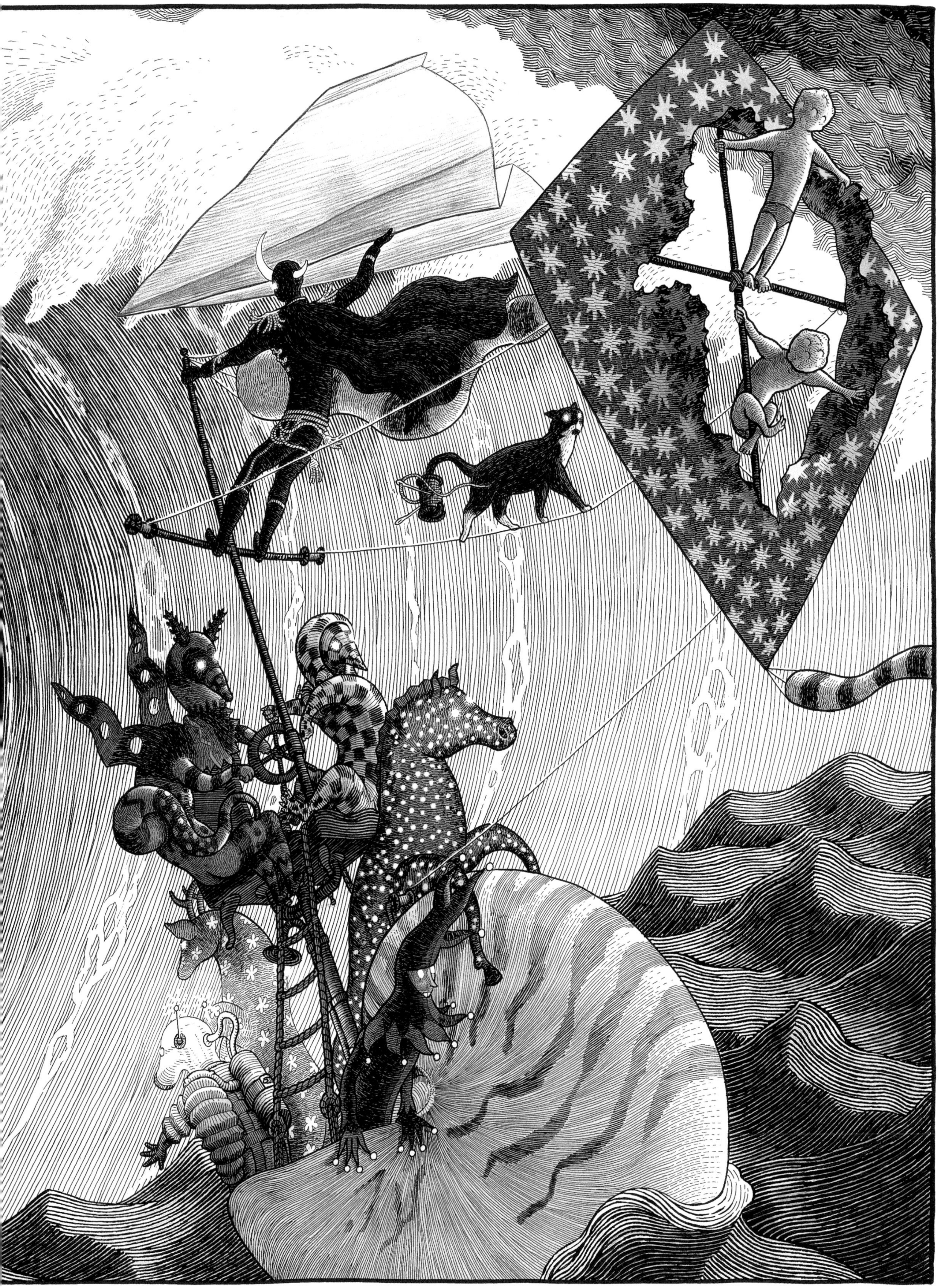

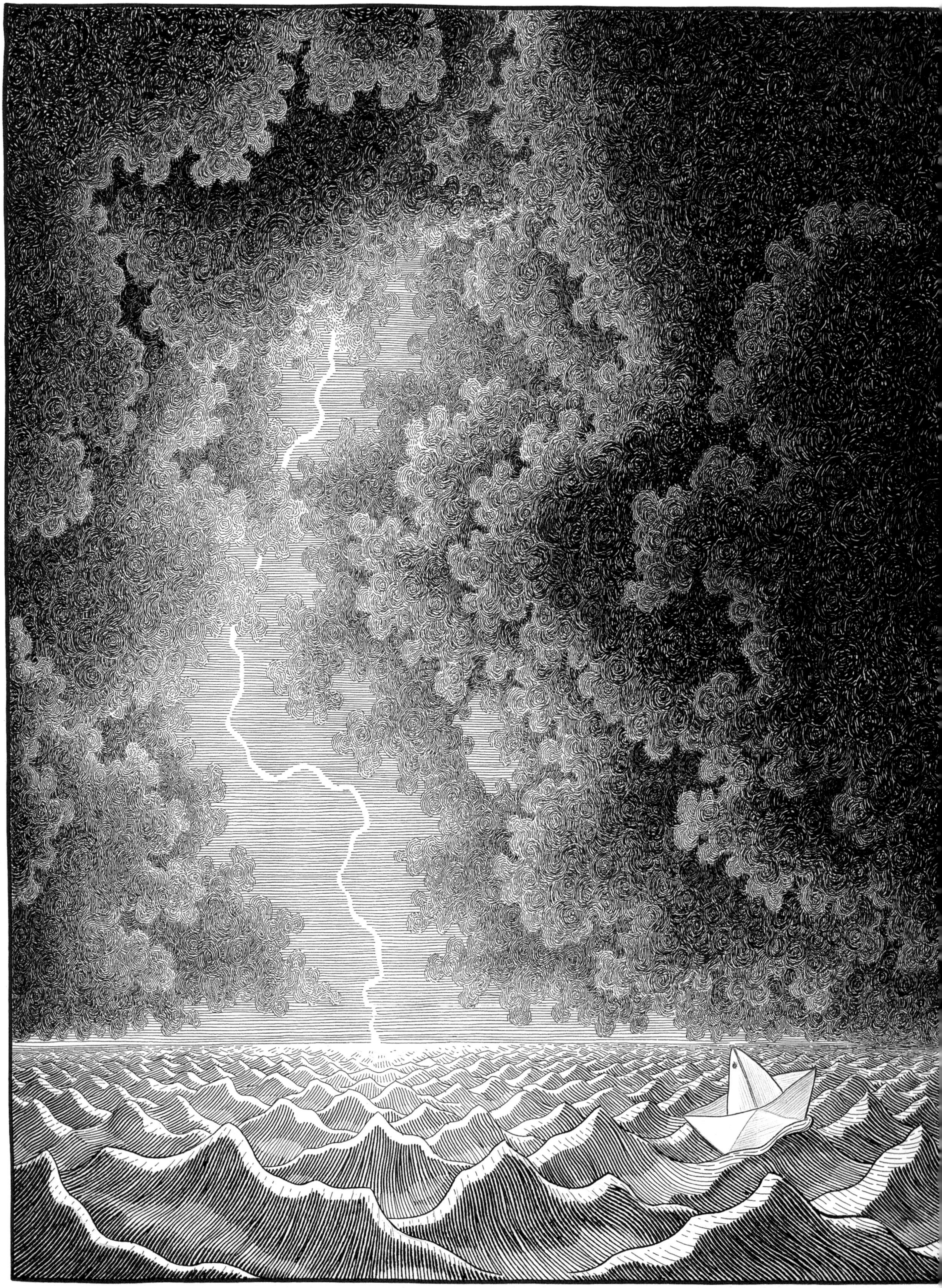

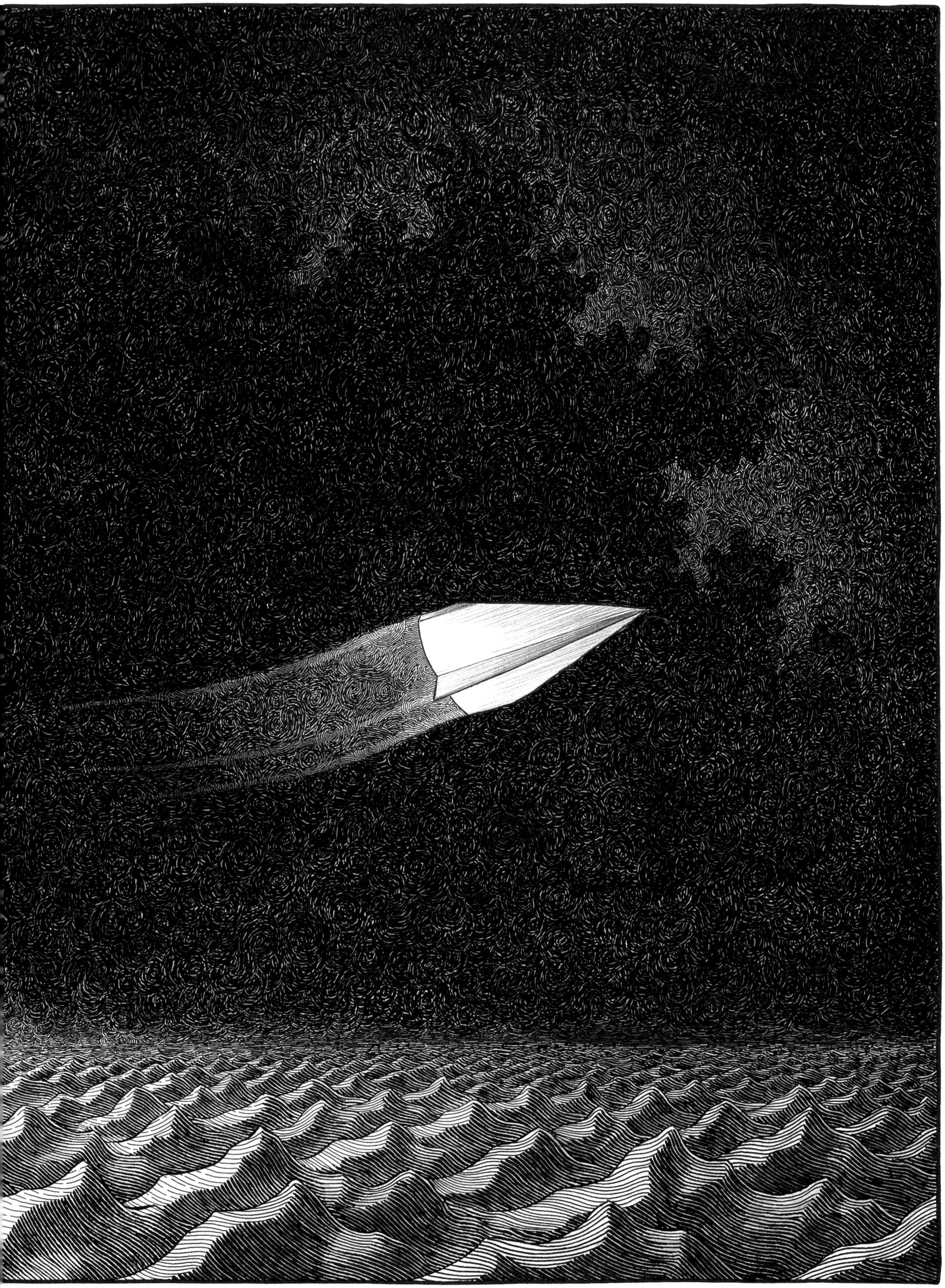

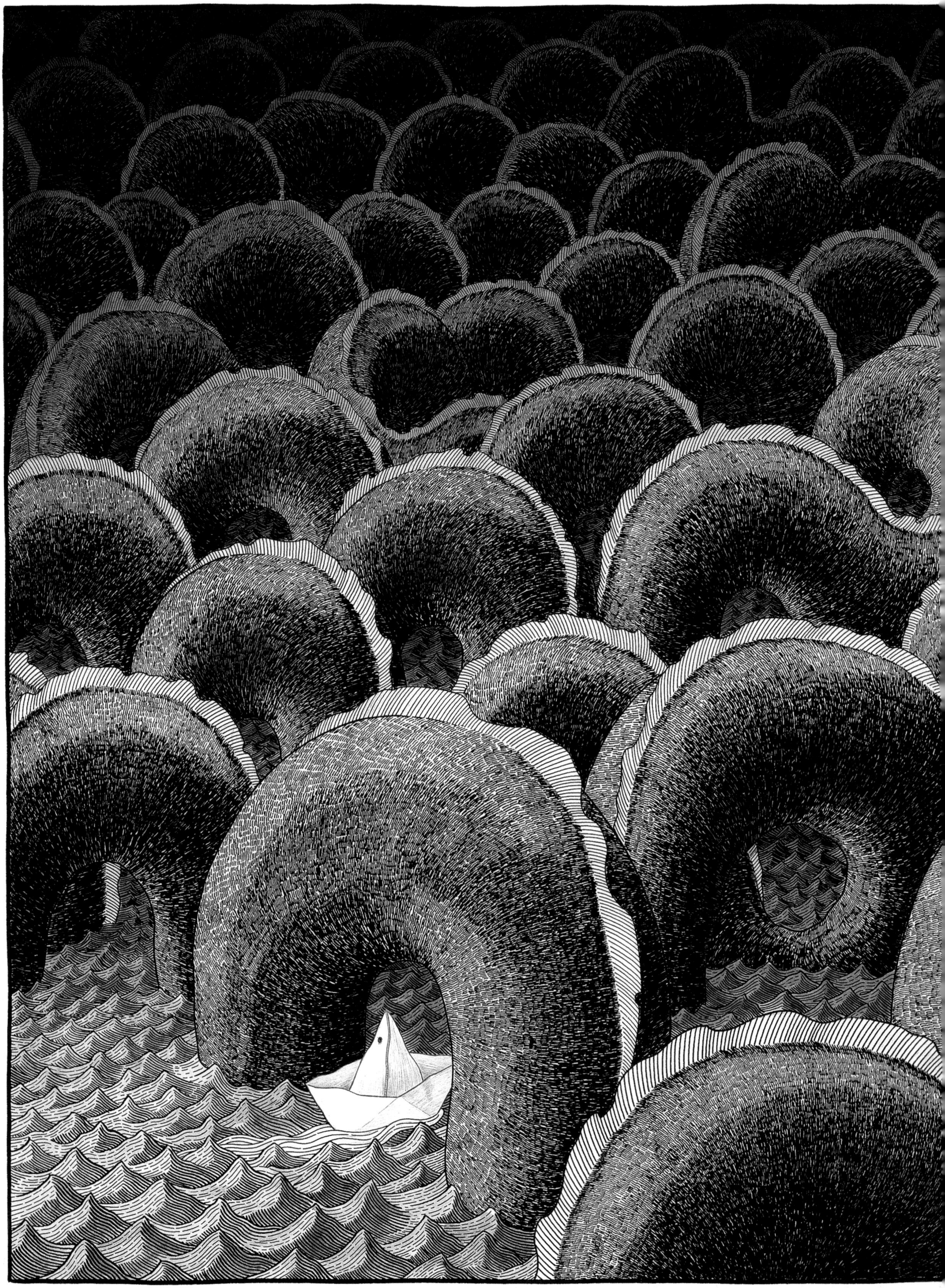

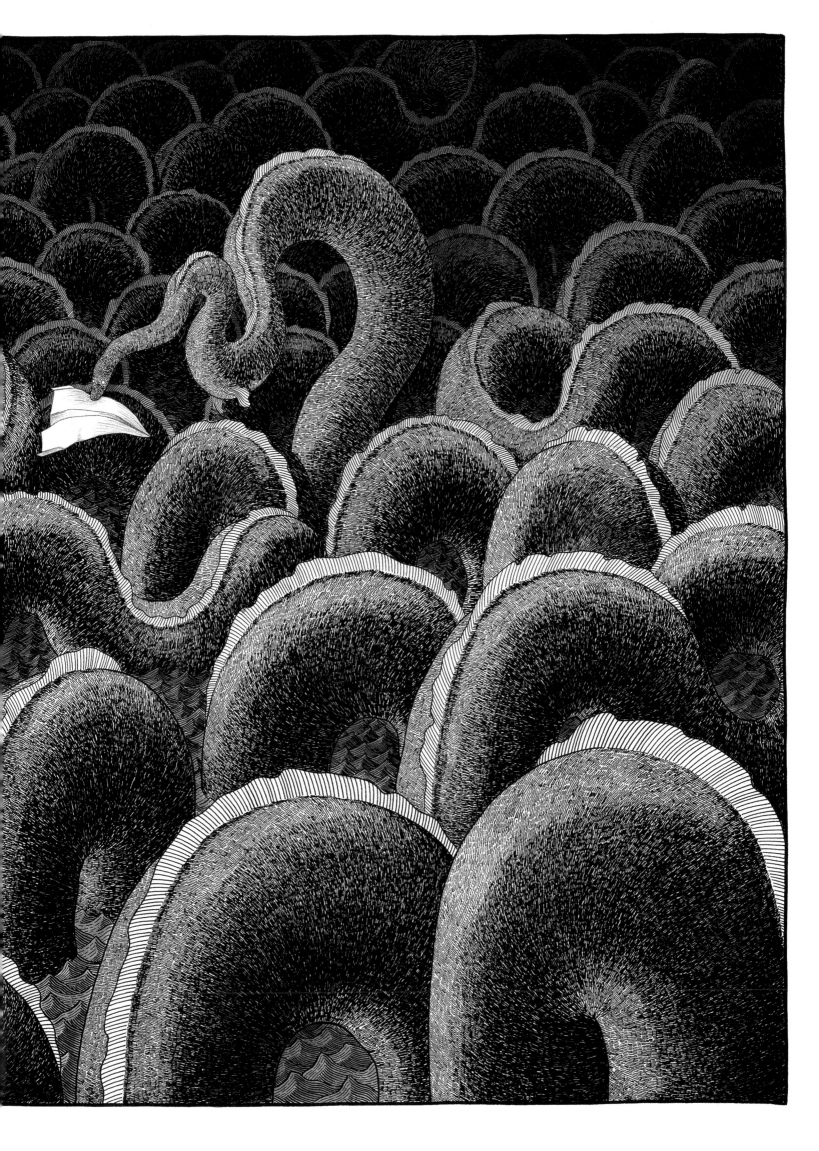

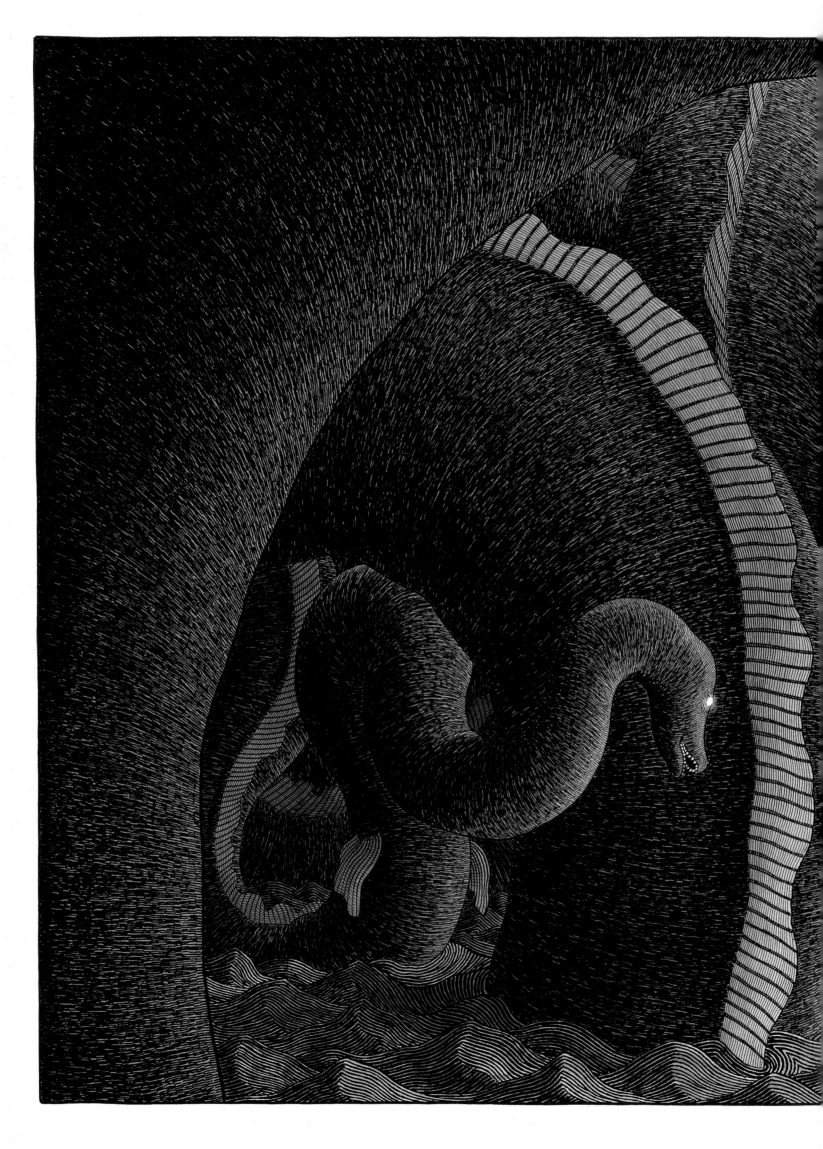

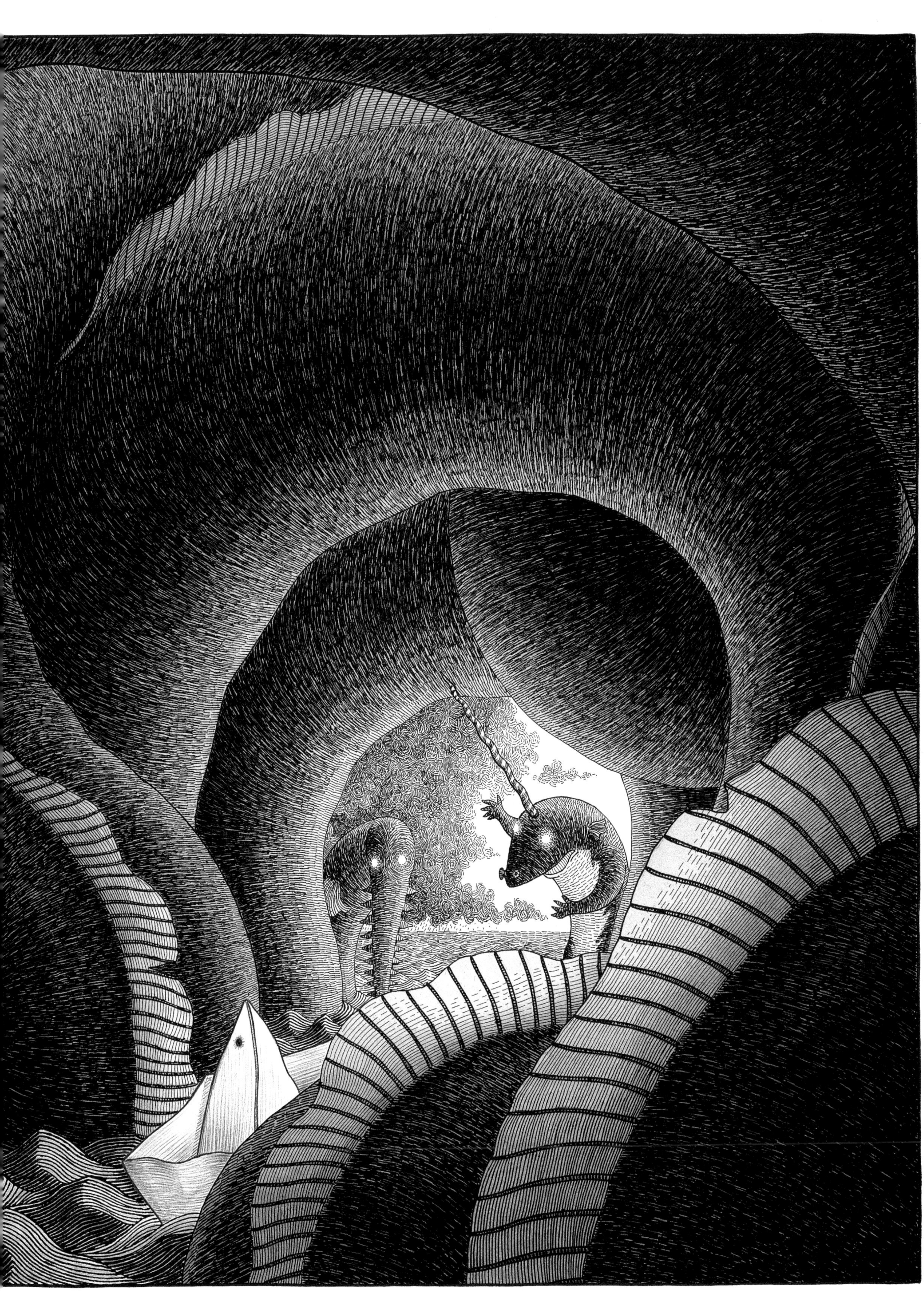

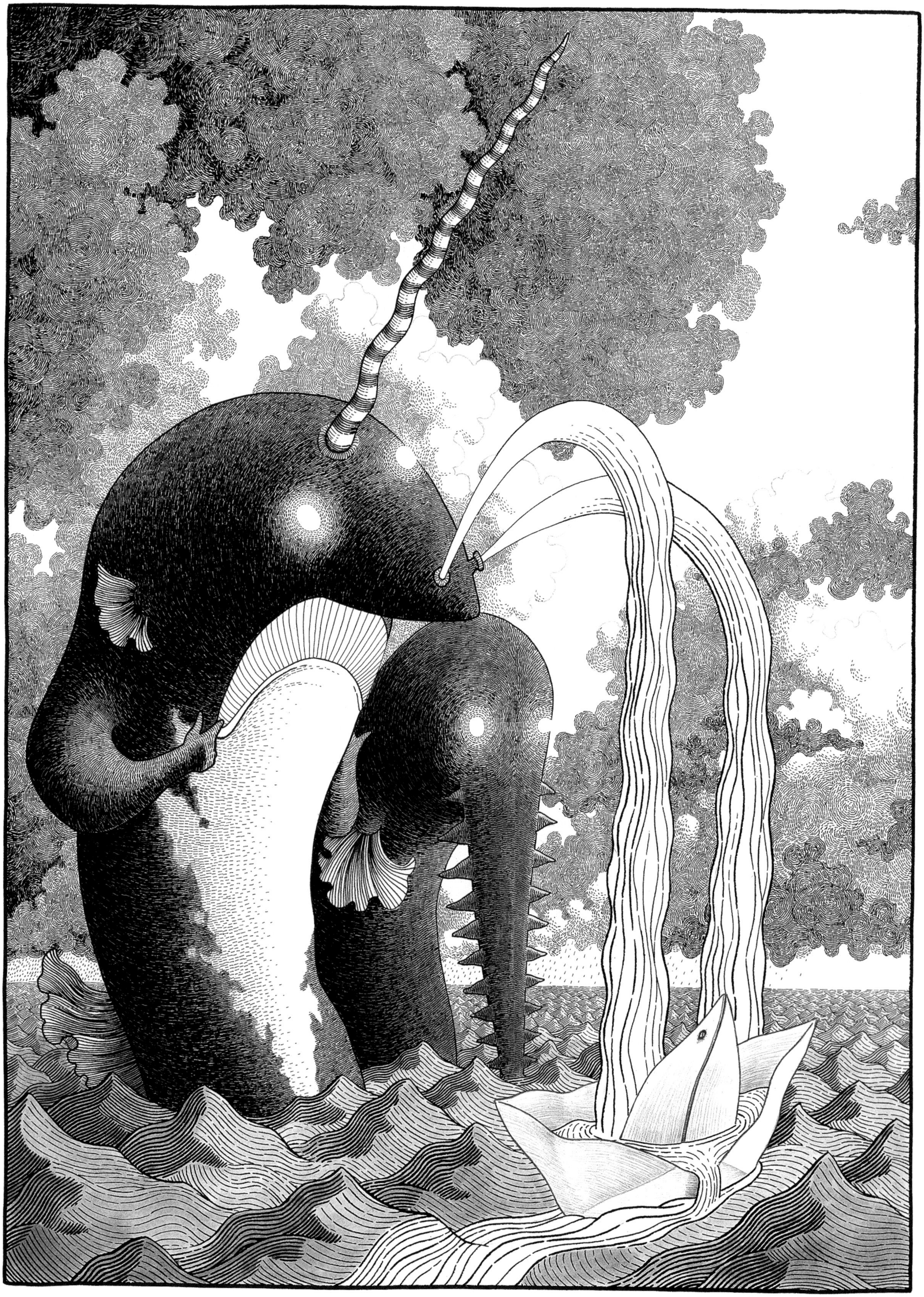

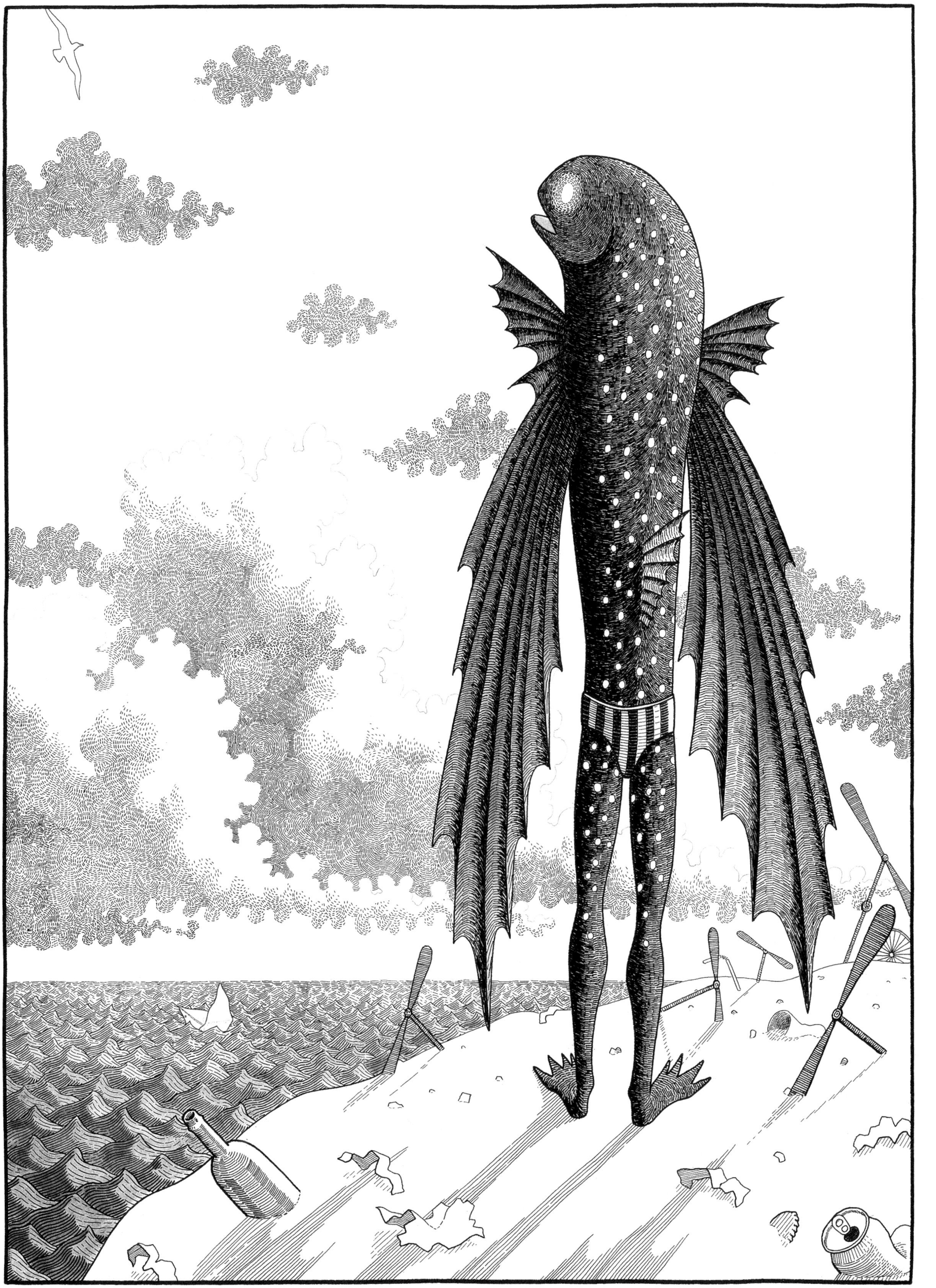

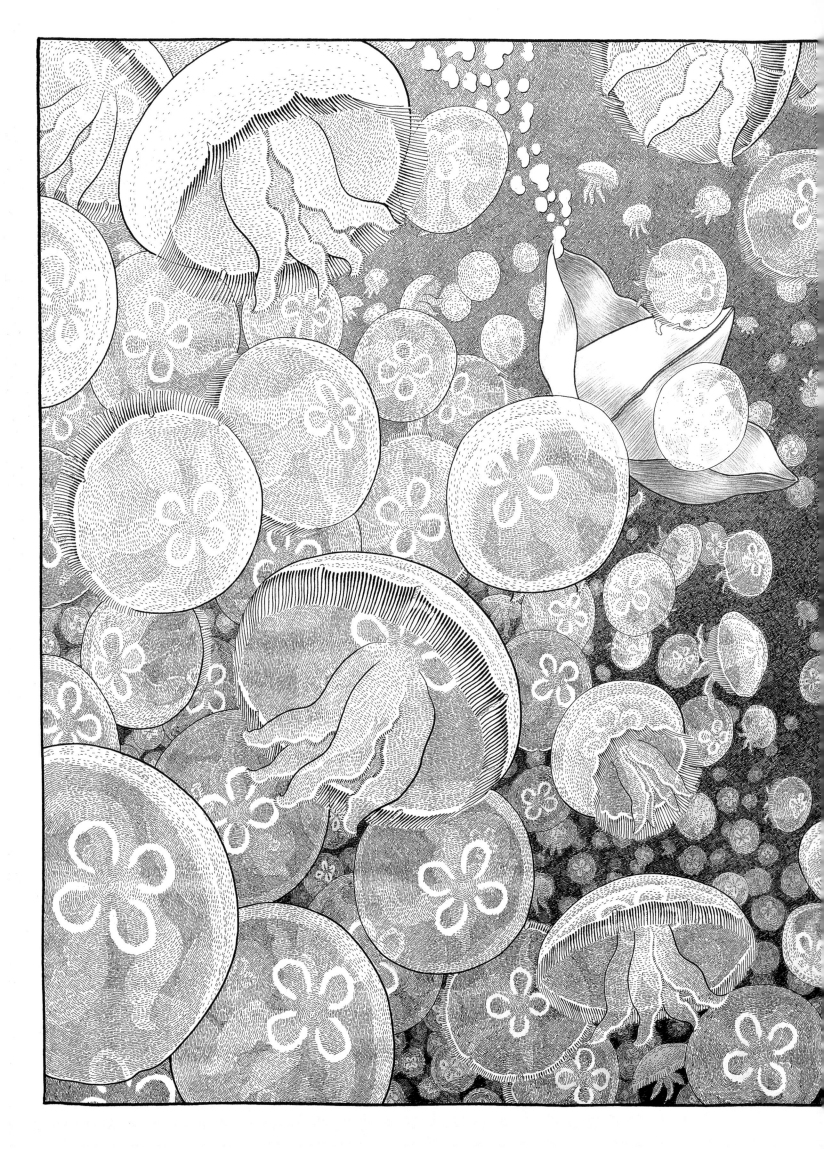

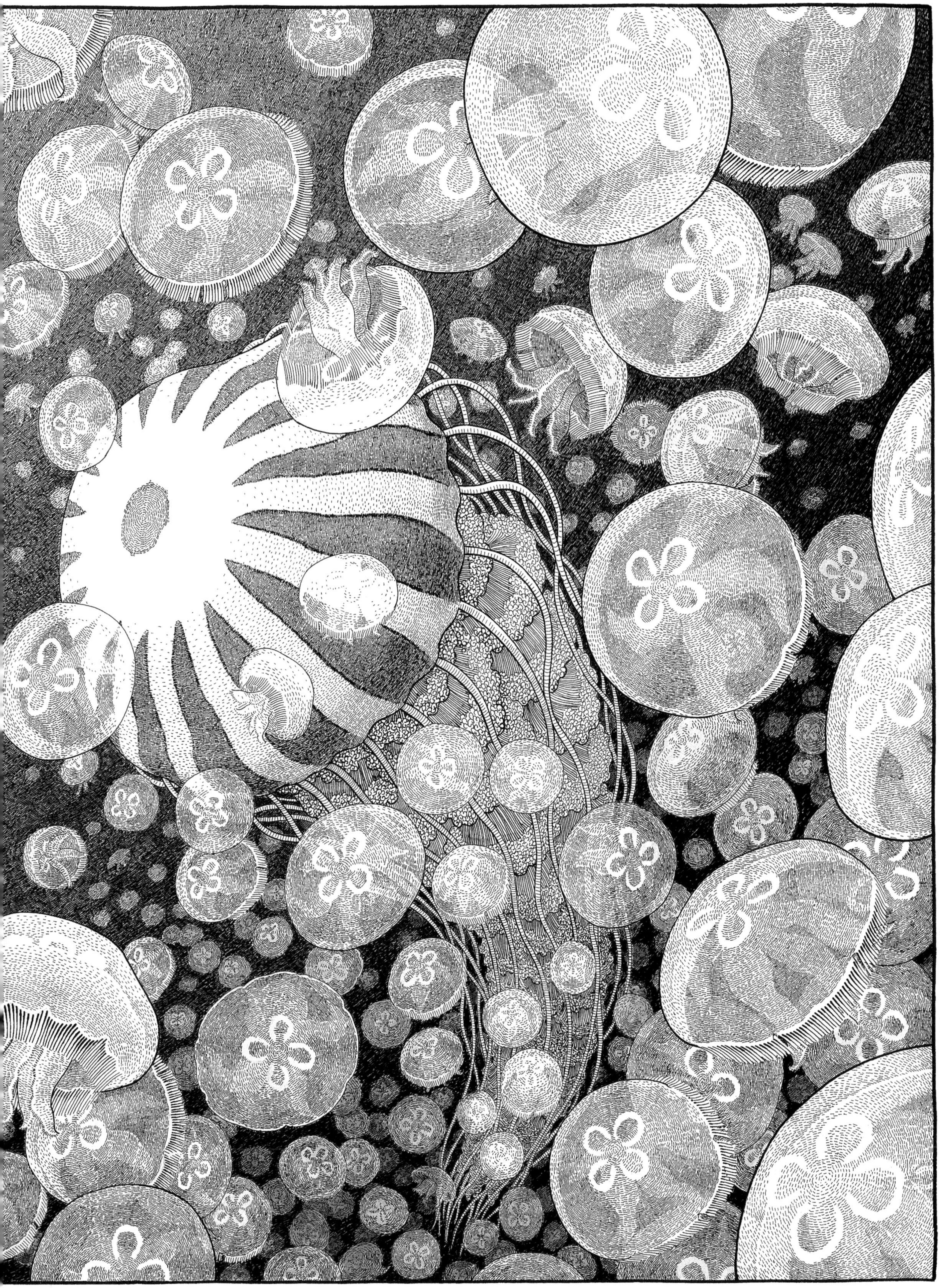

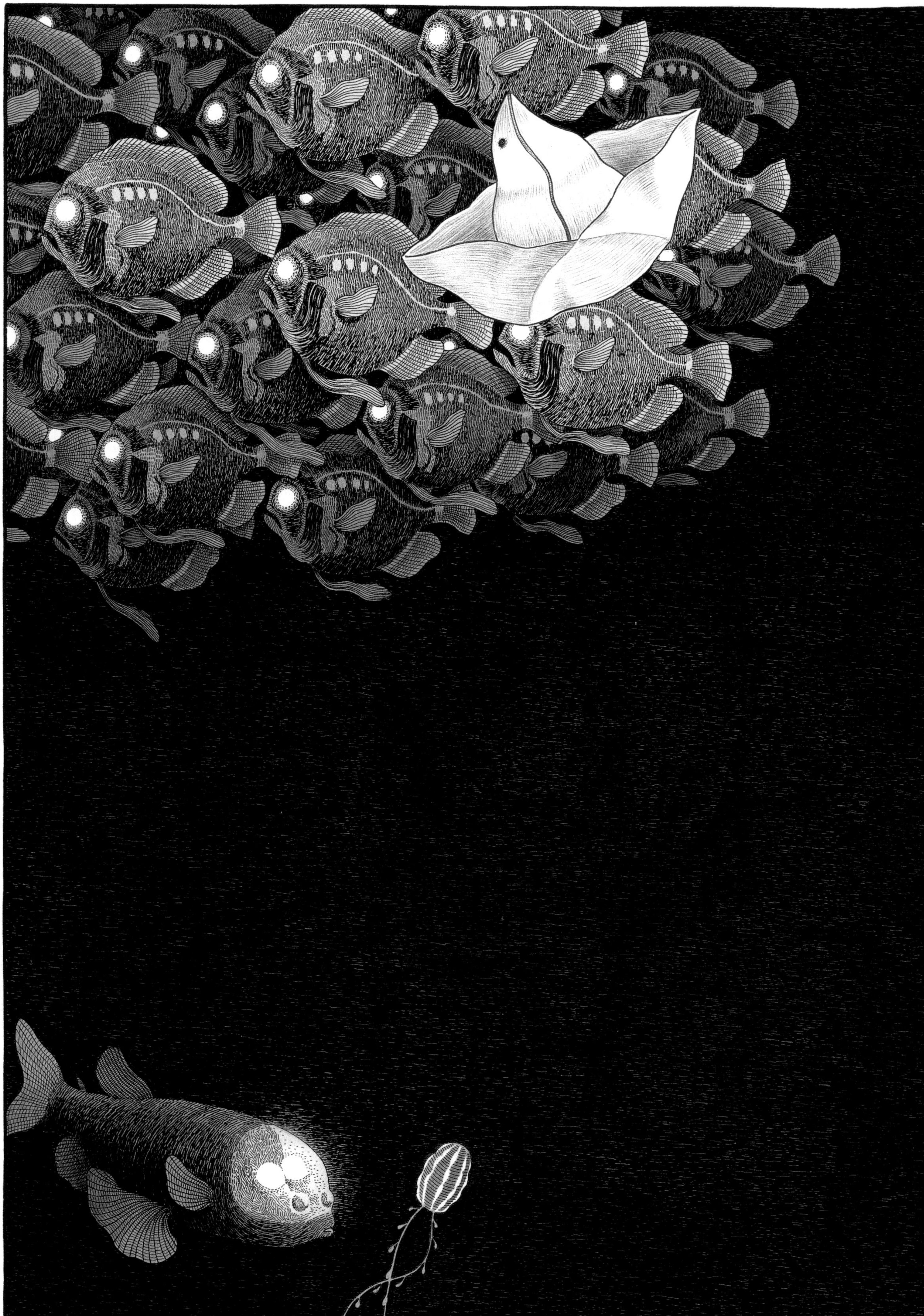

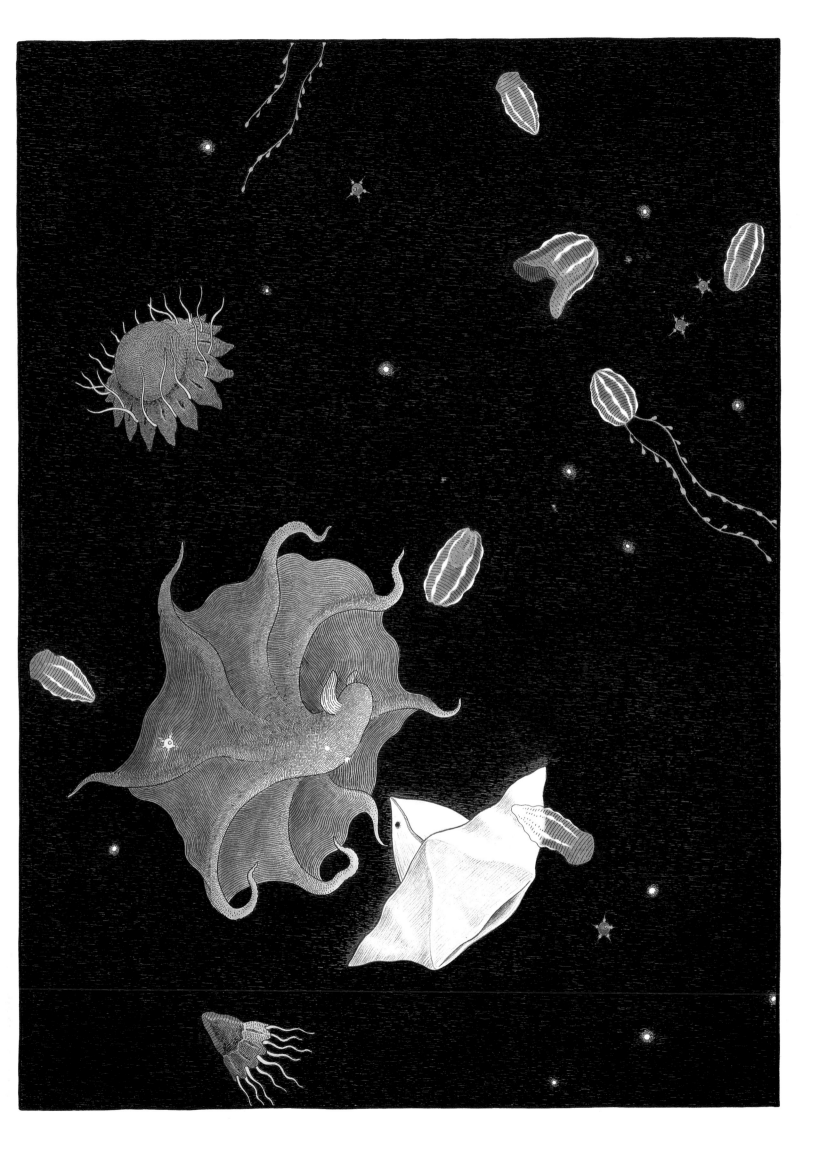

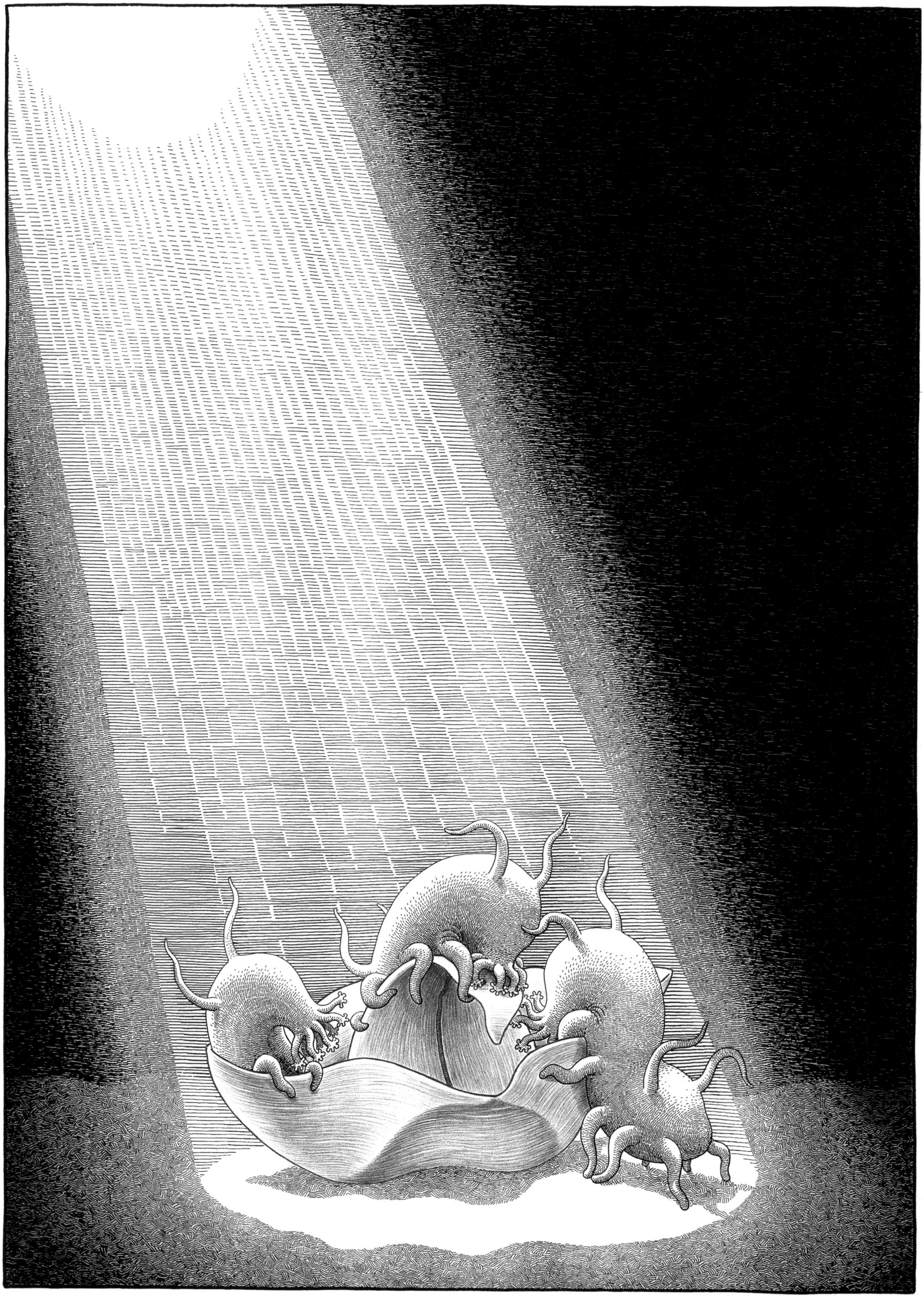

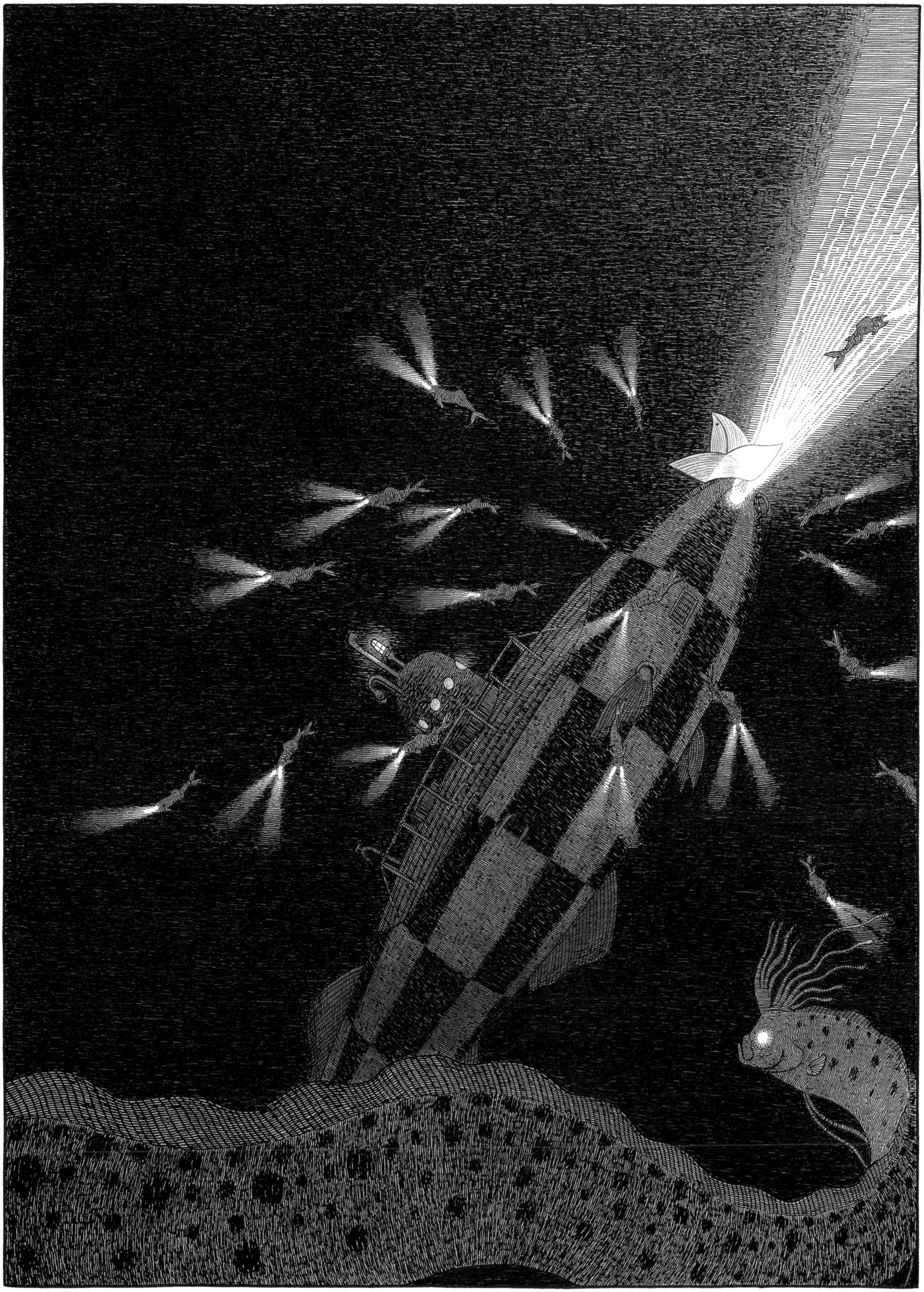

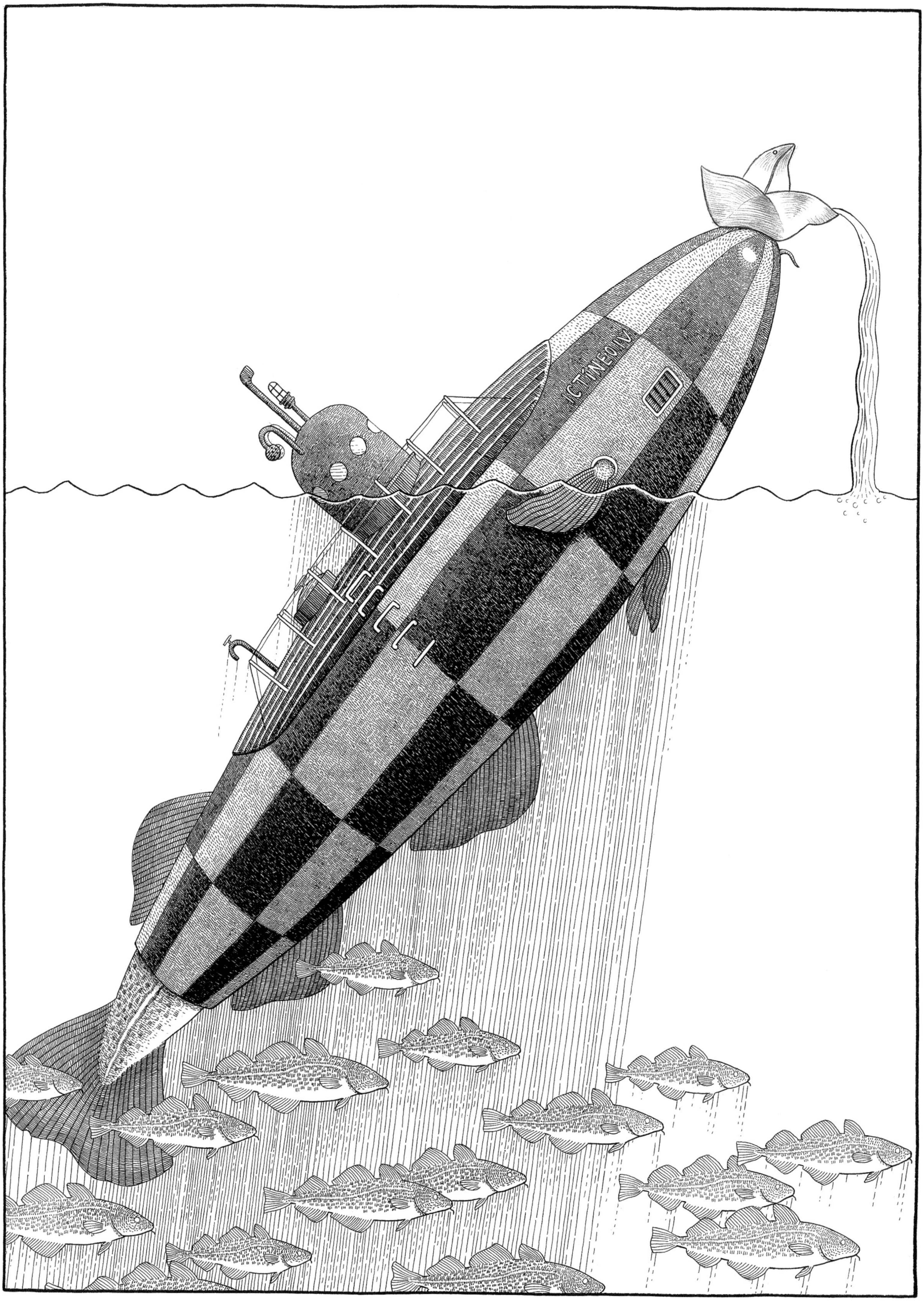
ICTÍNEO IV

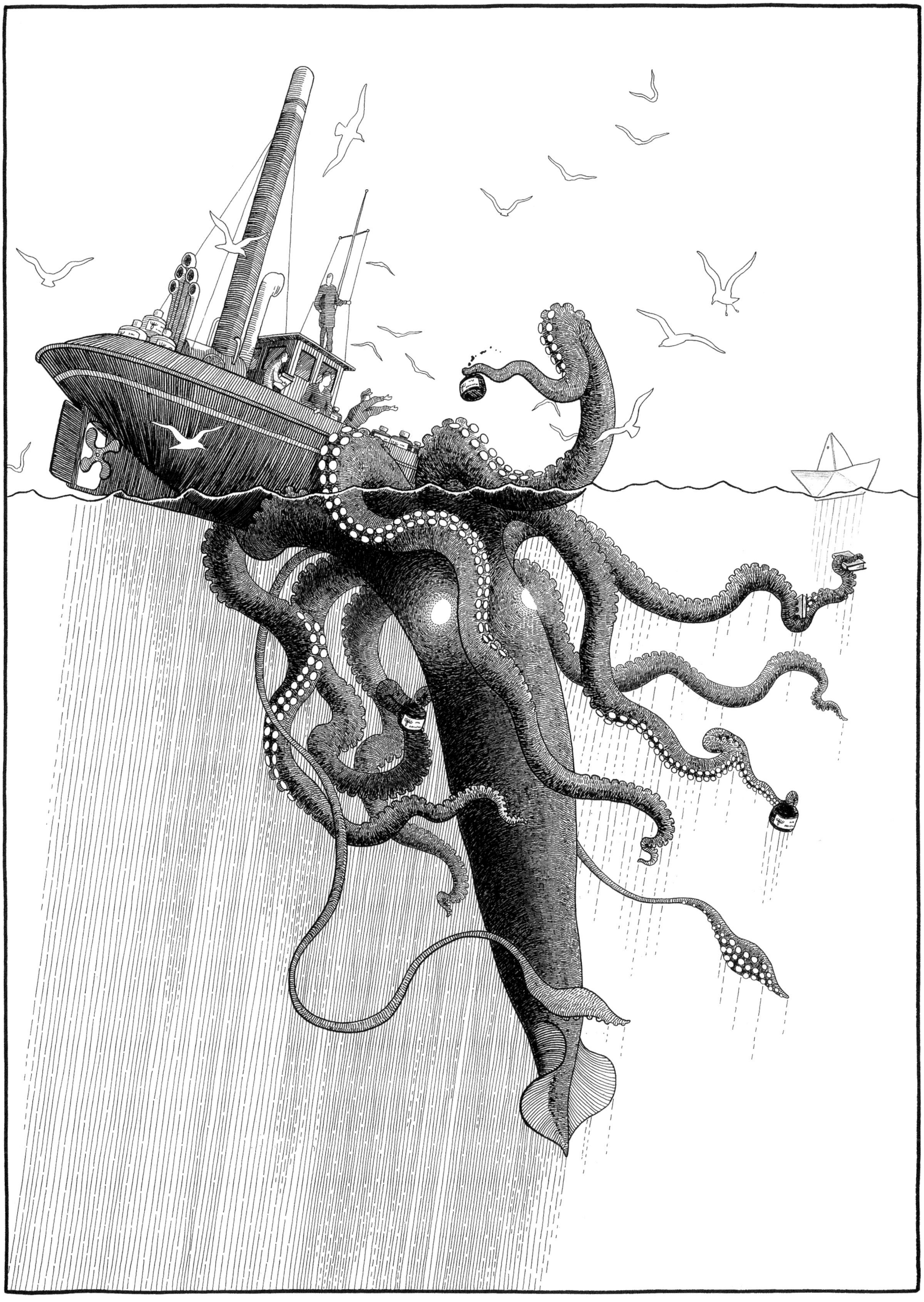

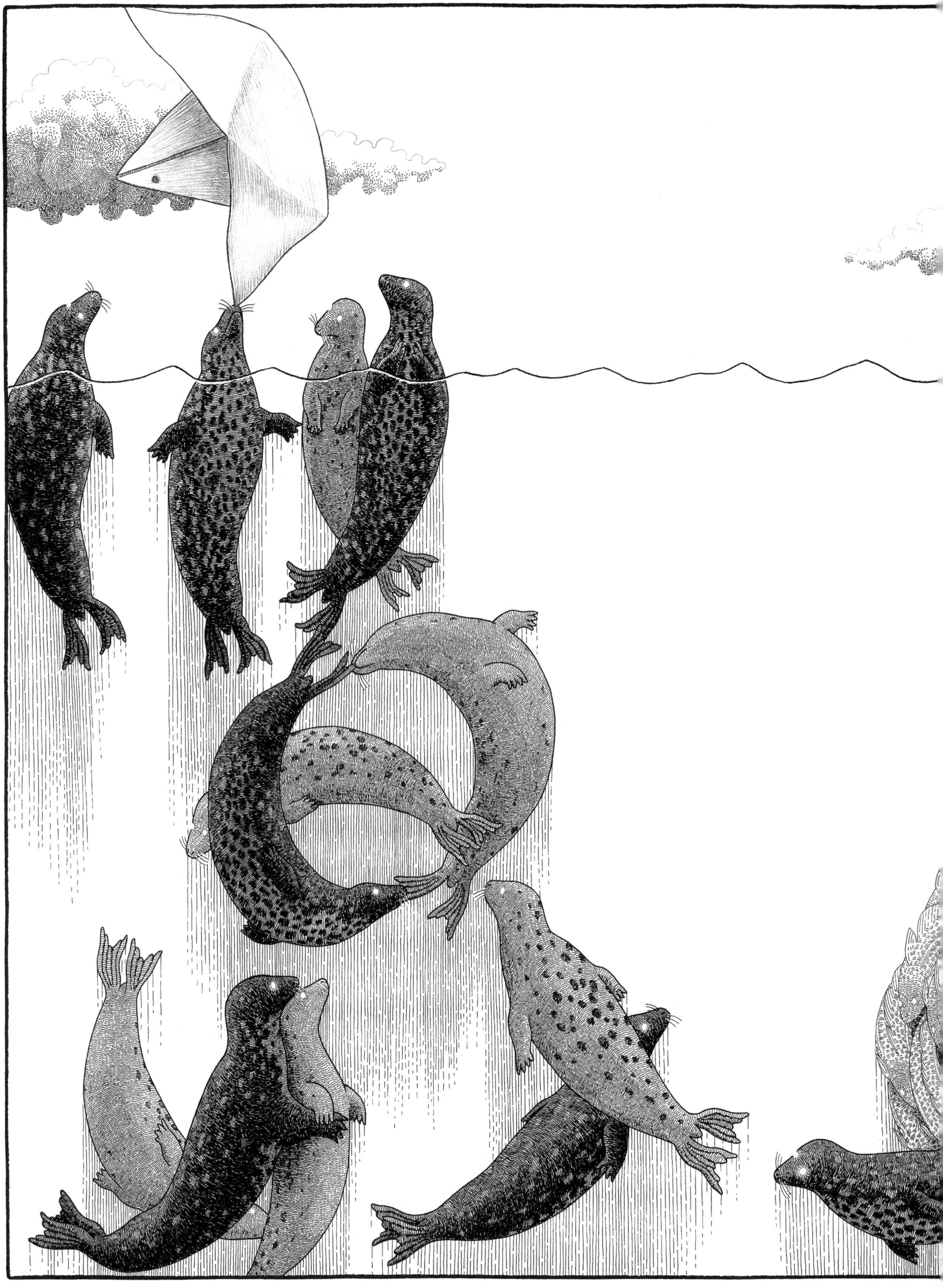

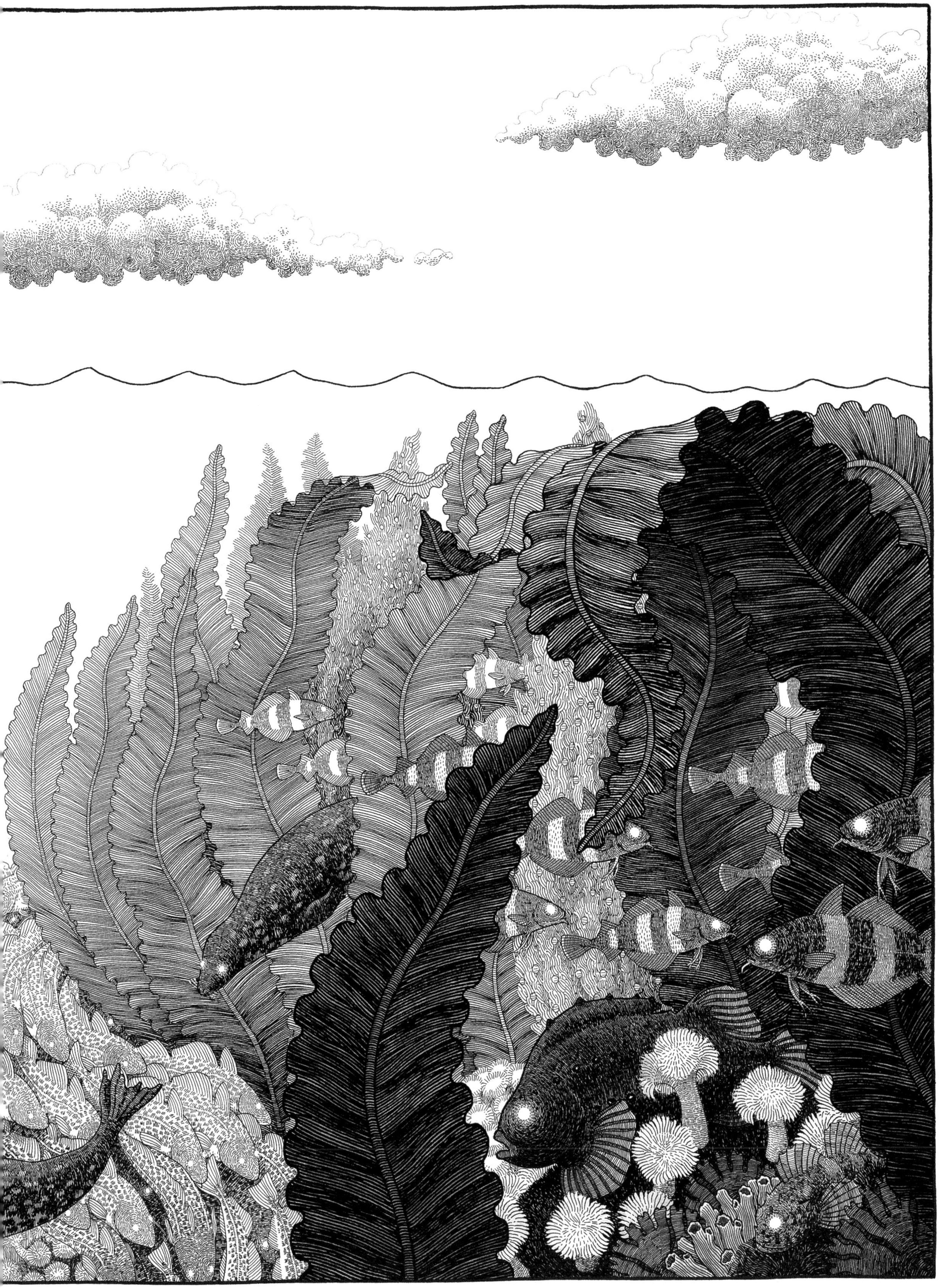

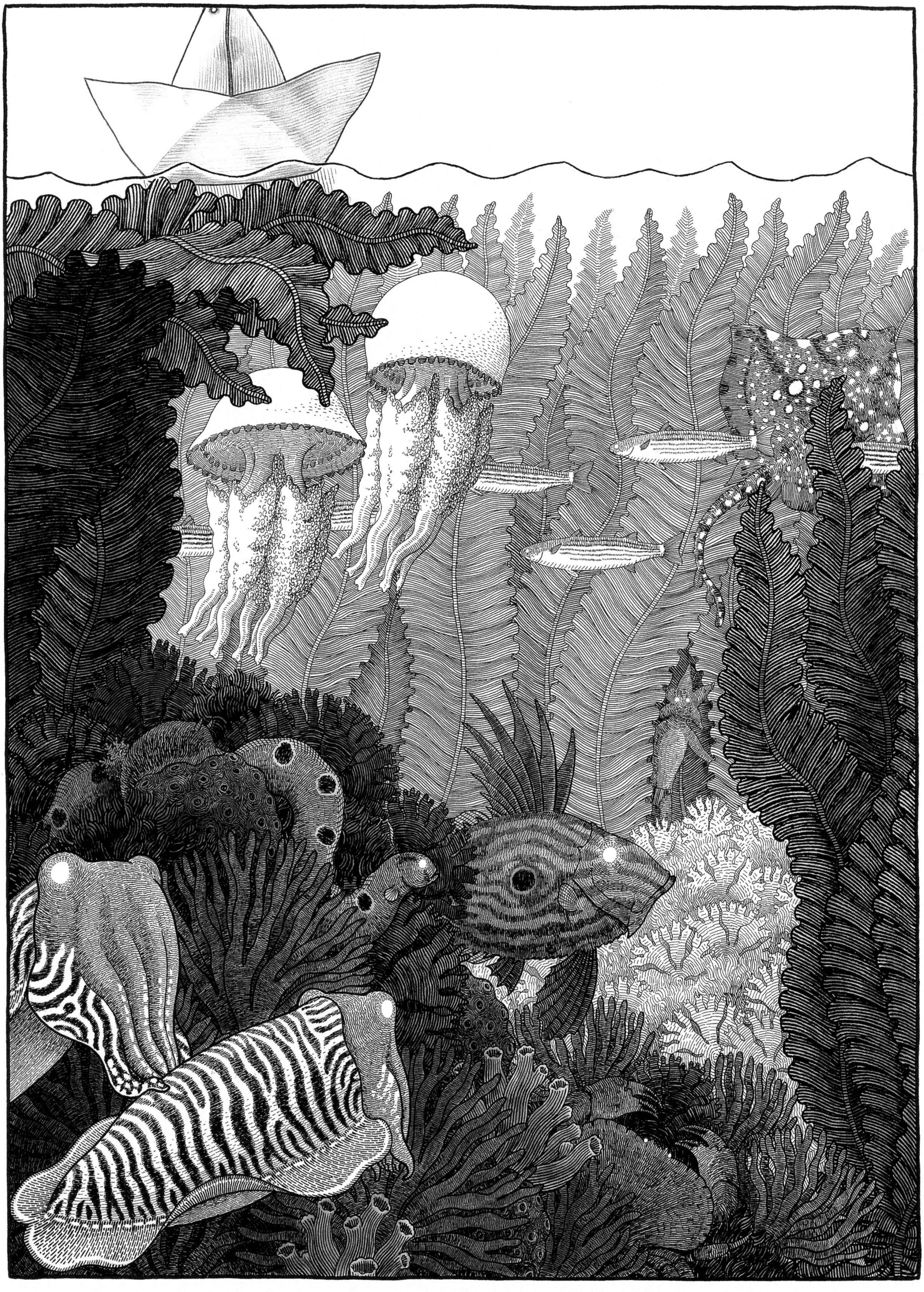

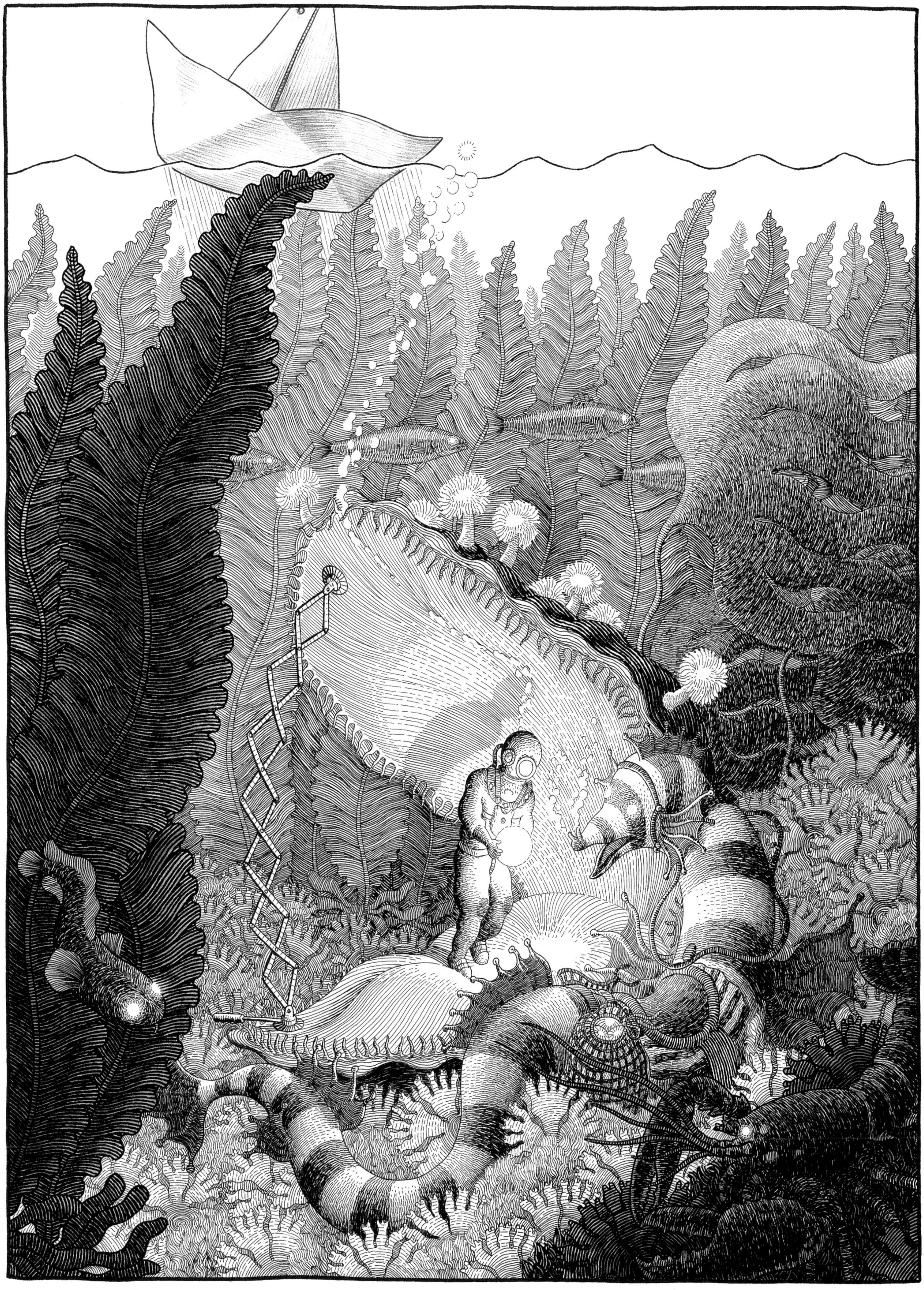

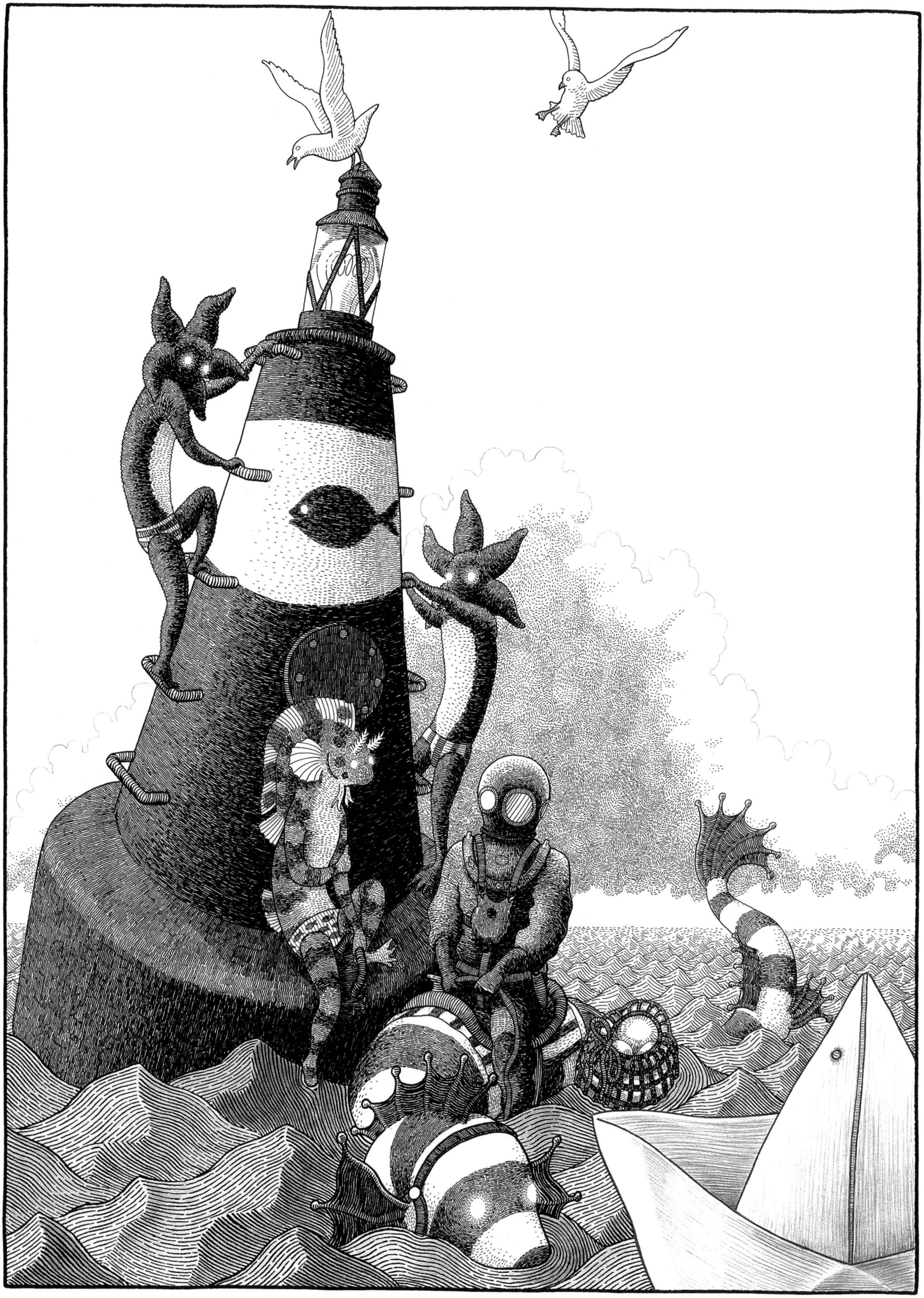

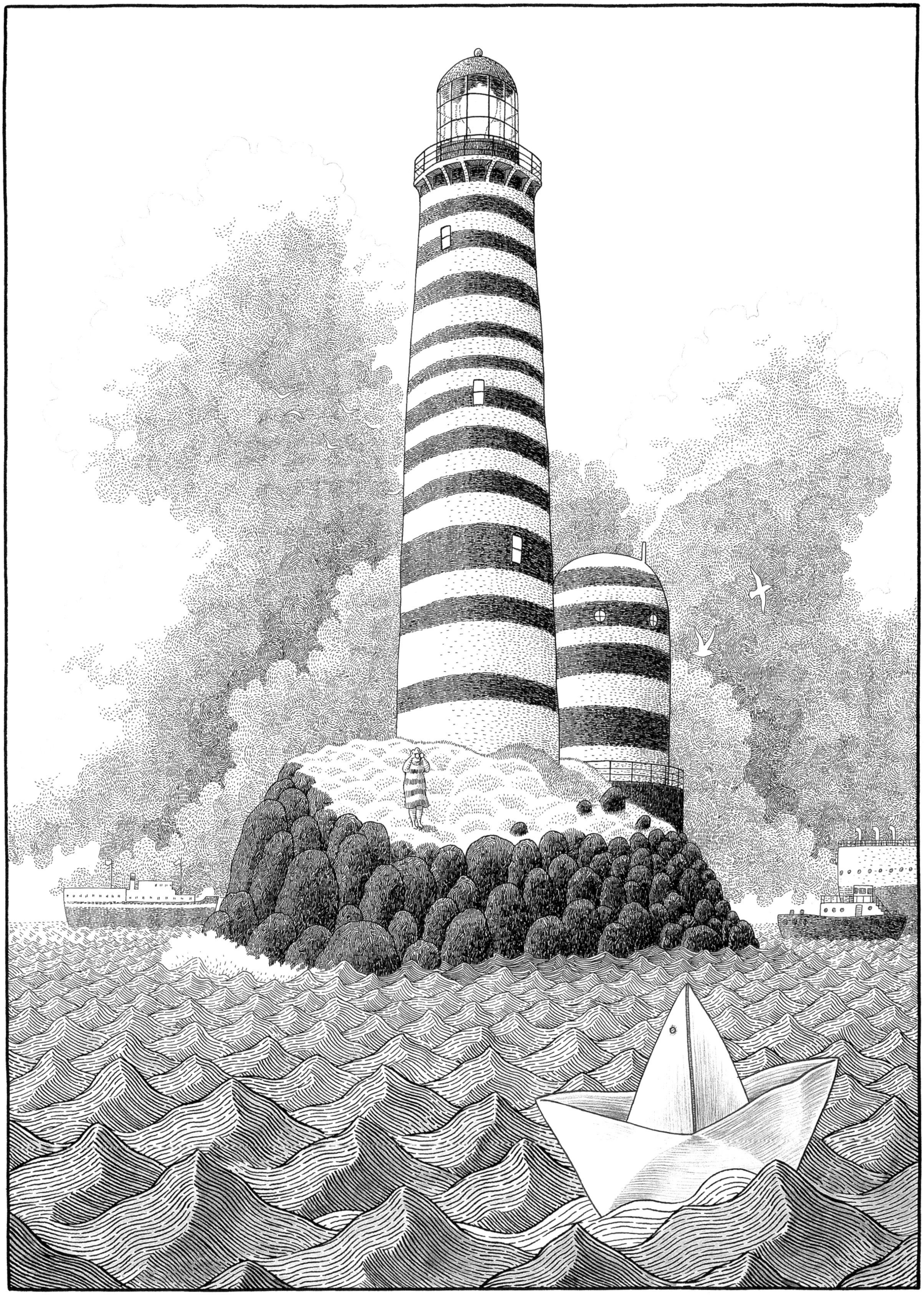

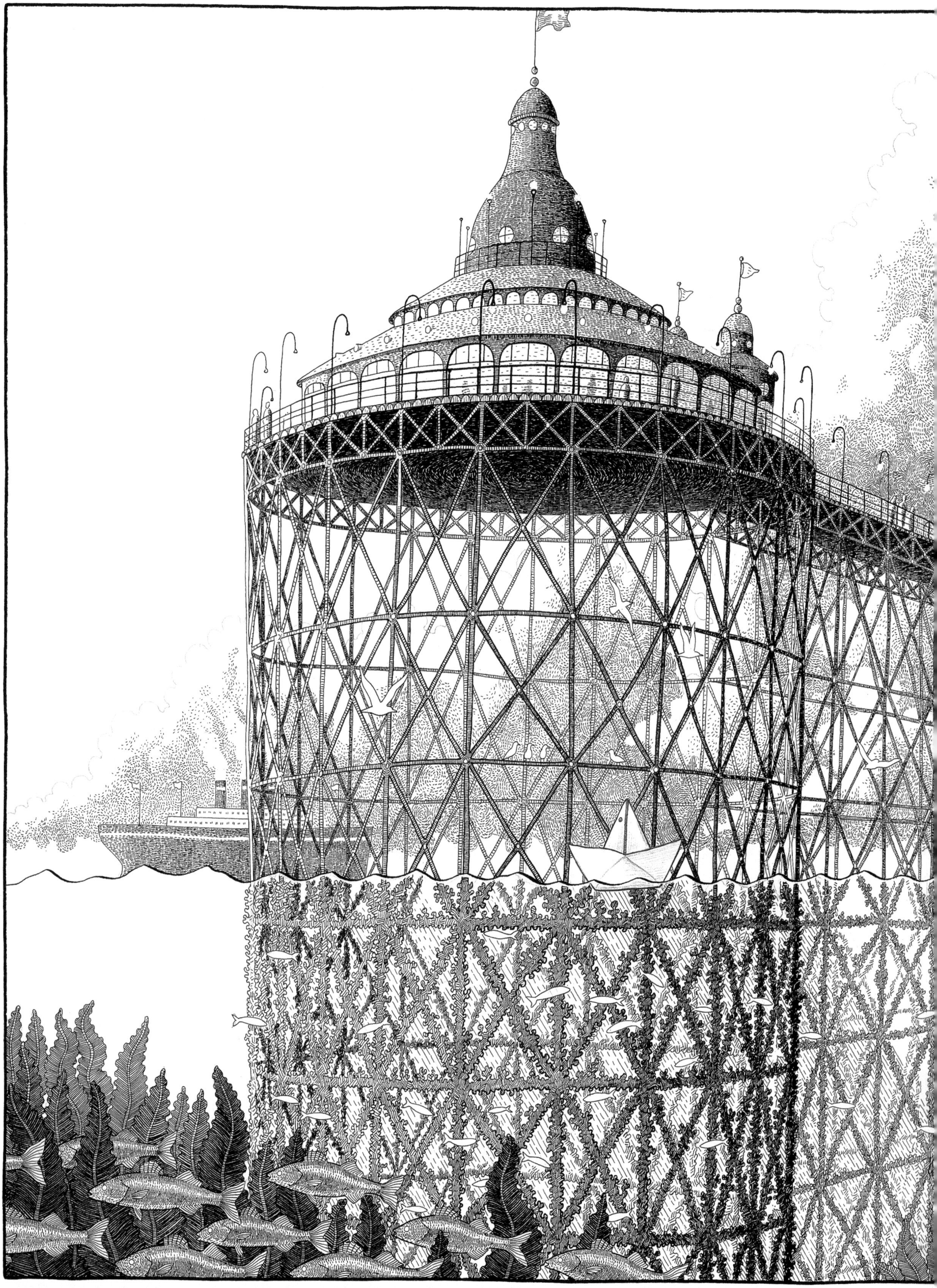

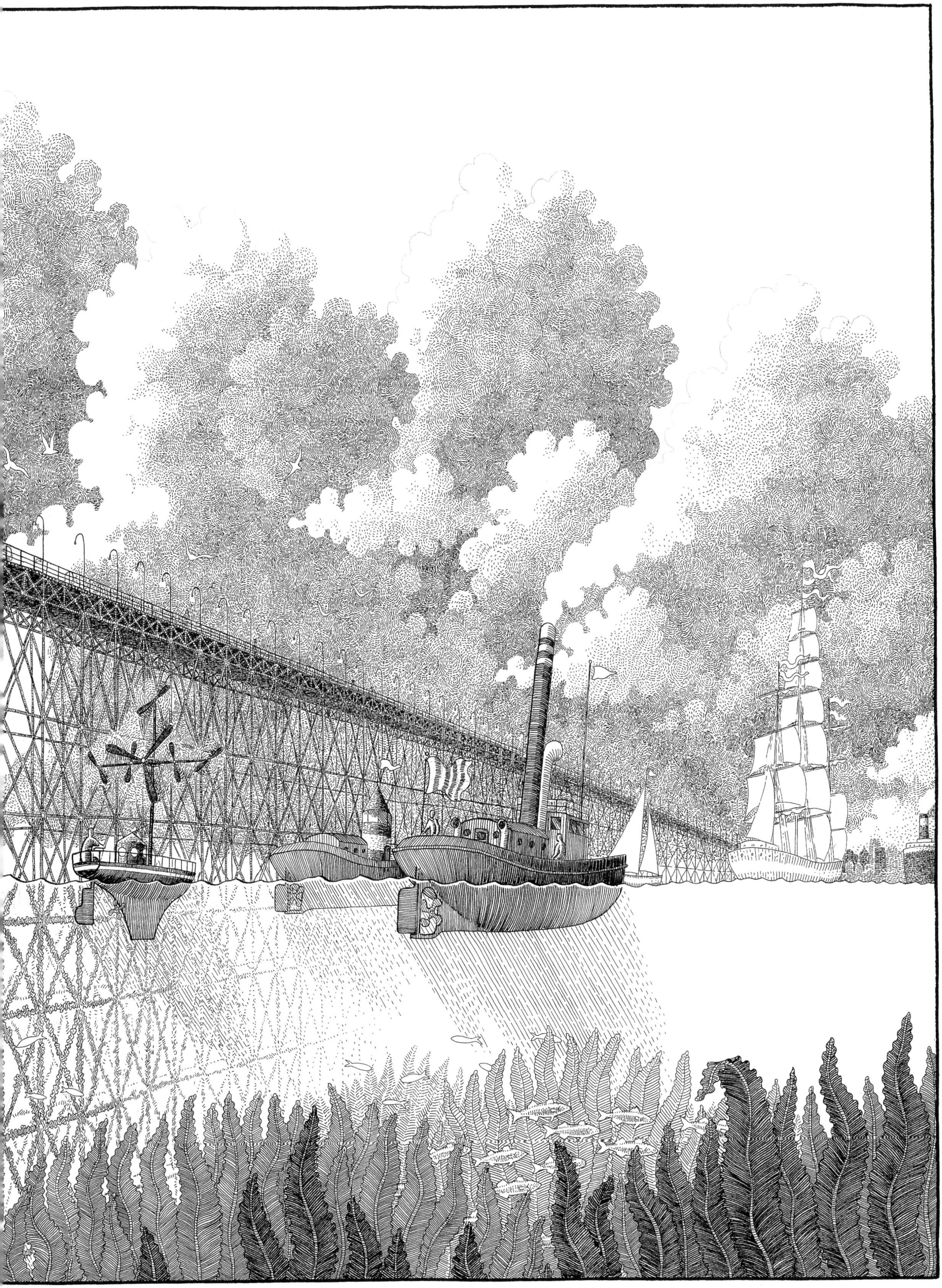

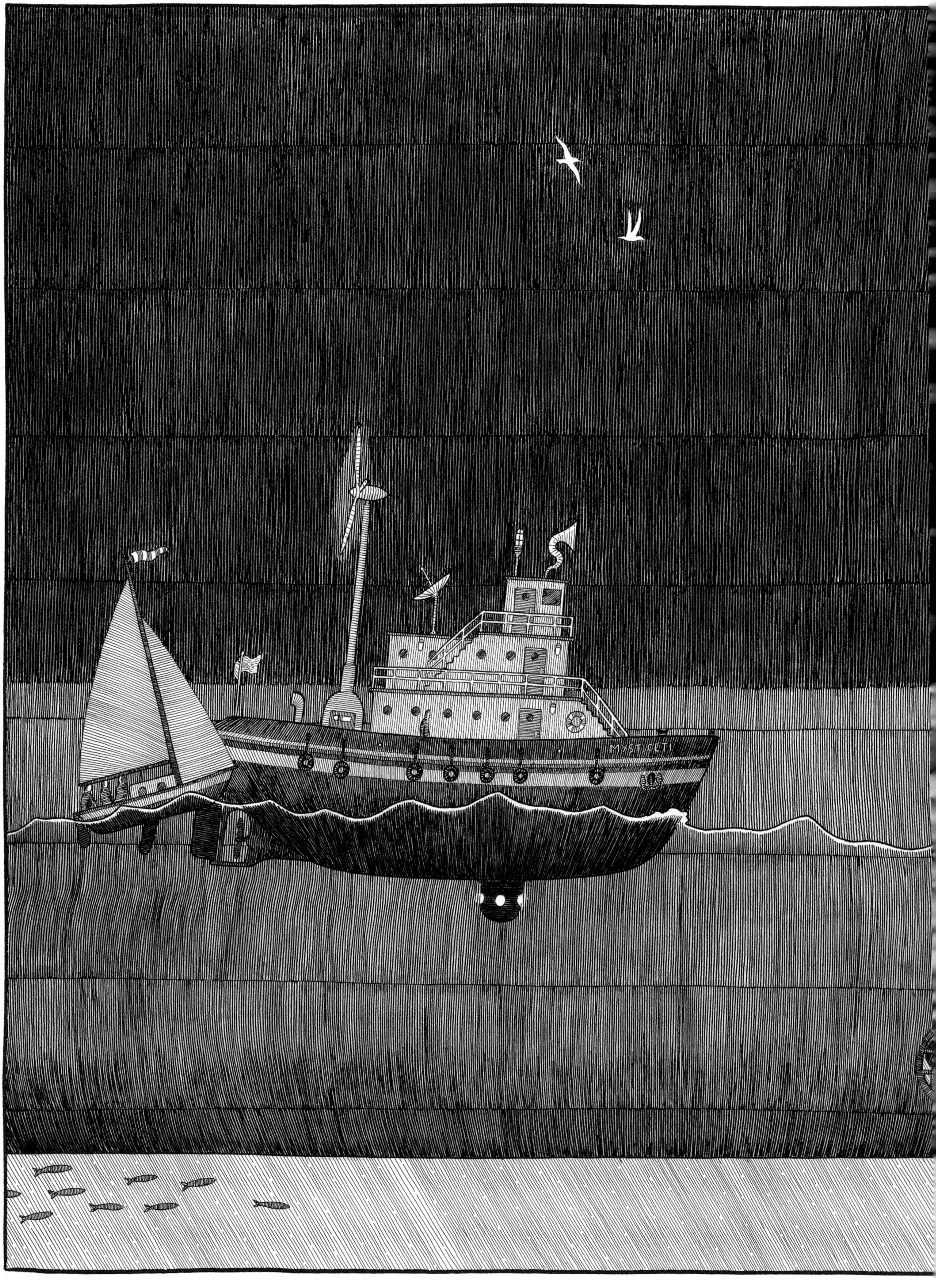
MYSTICETI

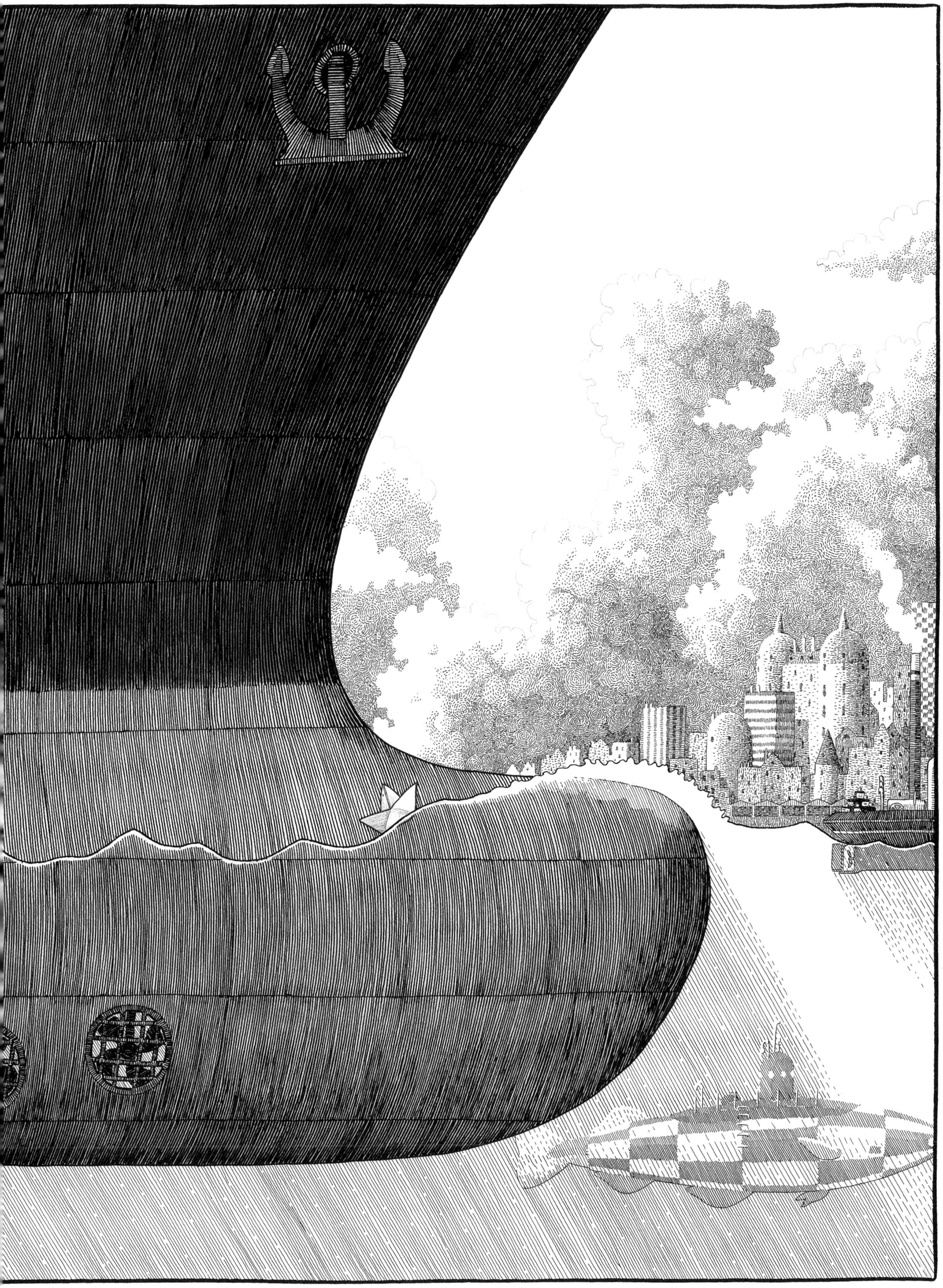

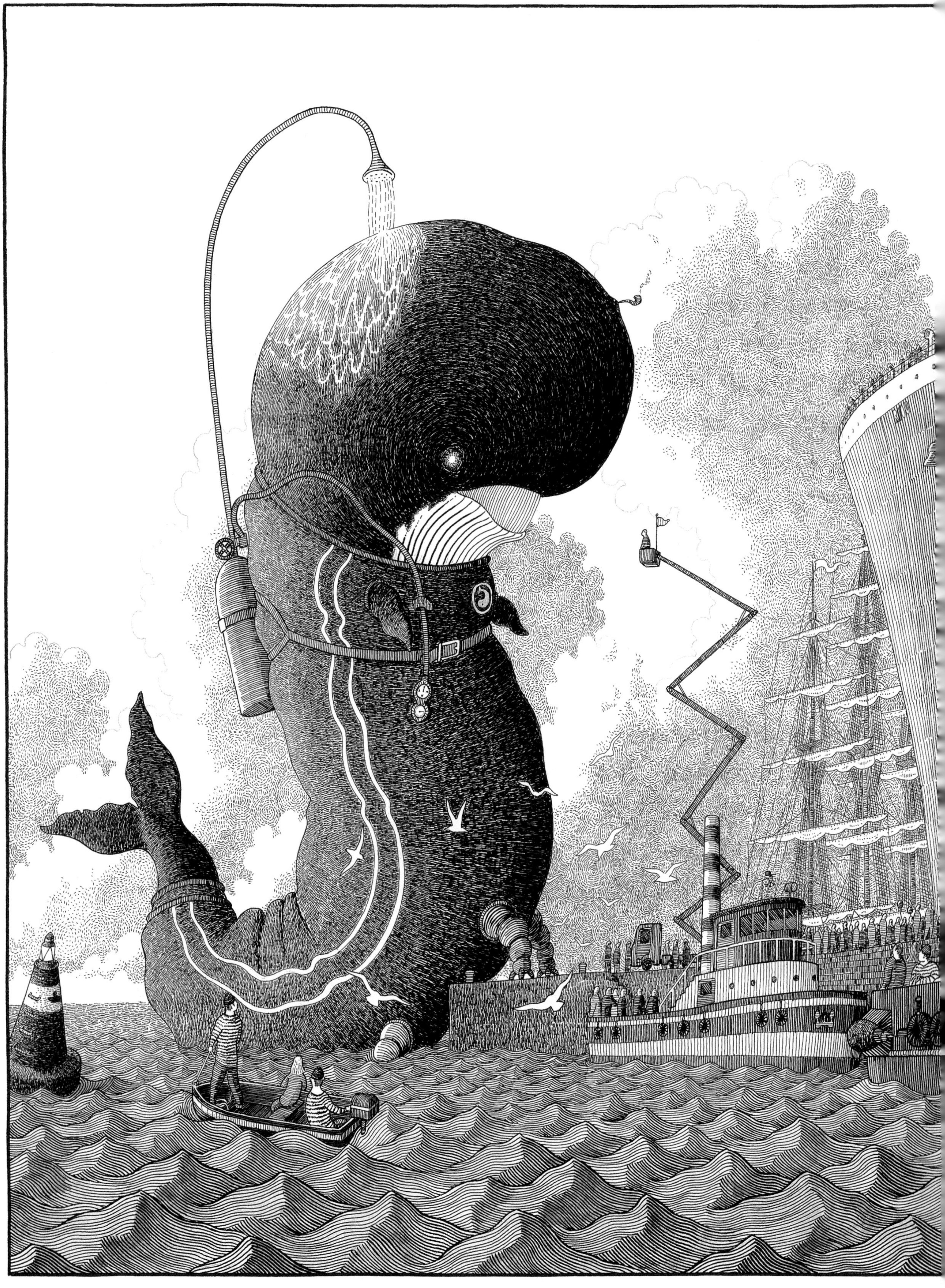

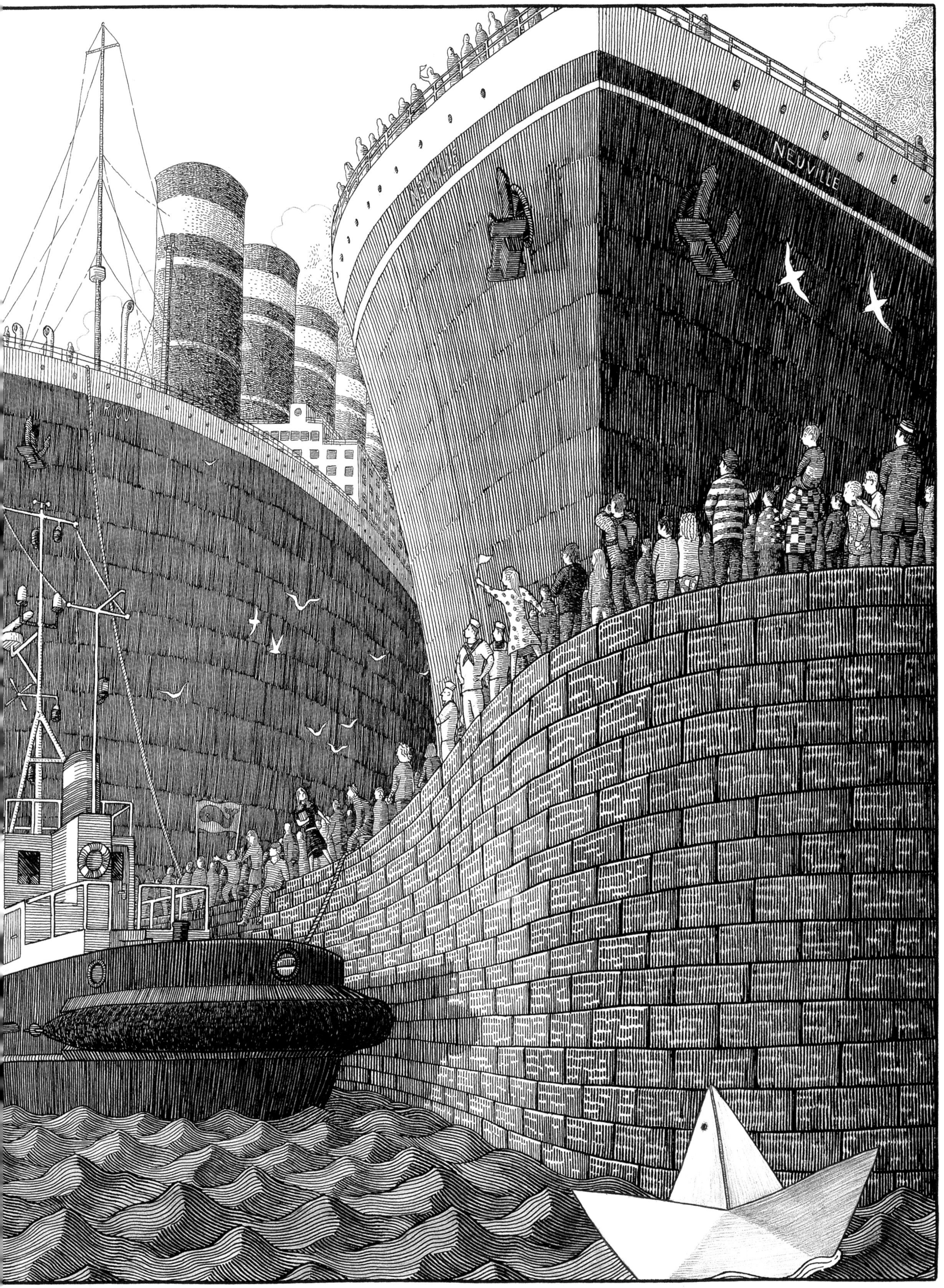
NEUVILLE
NEUVILLE
RIOU

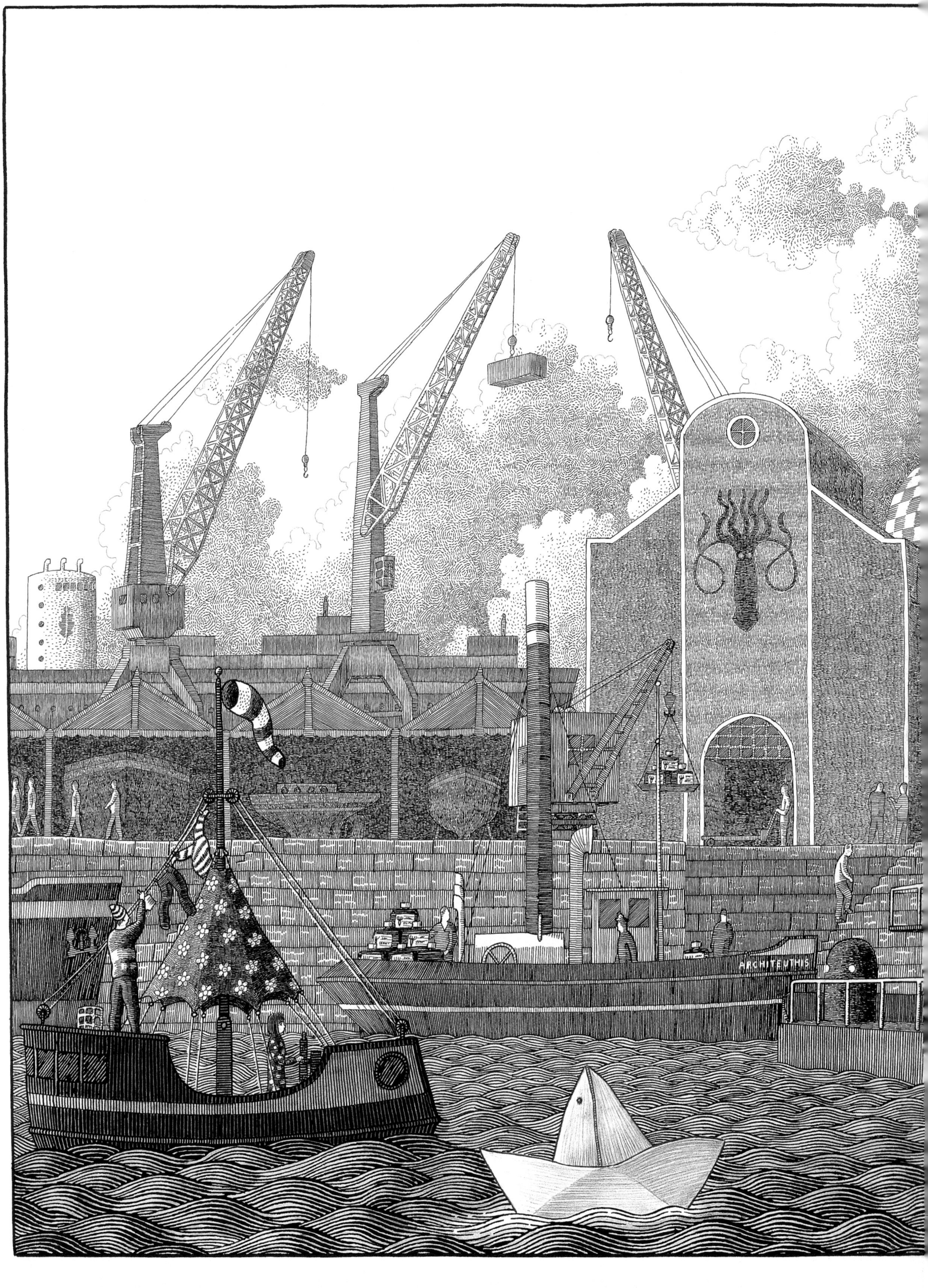
ARCHITEUTHIS

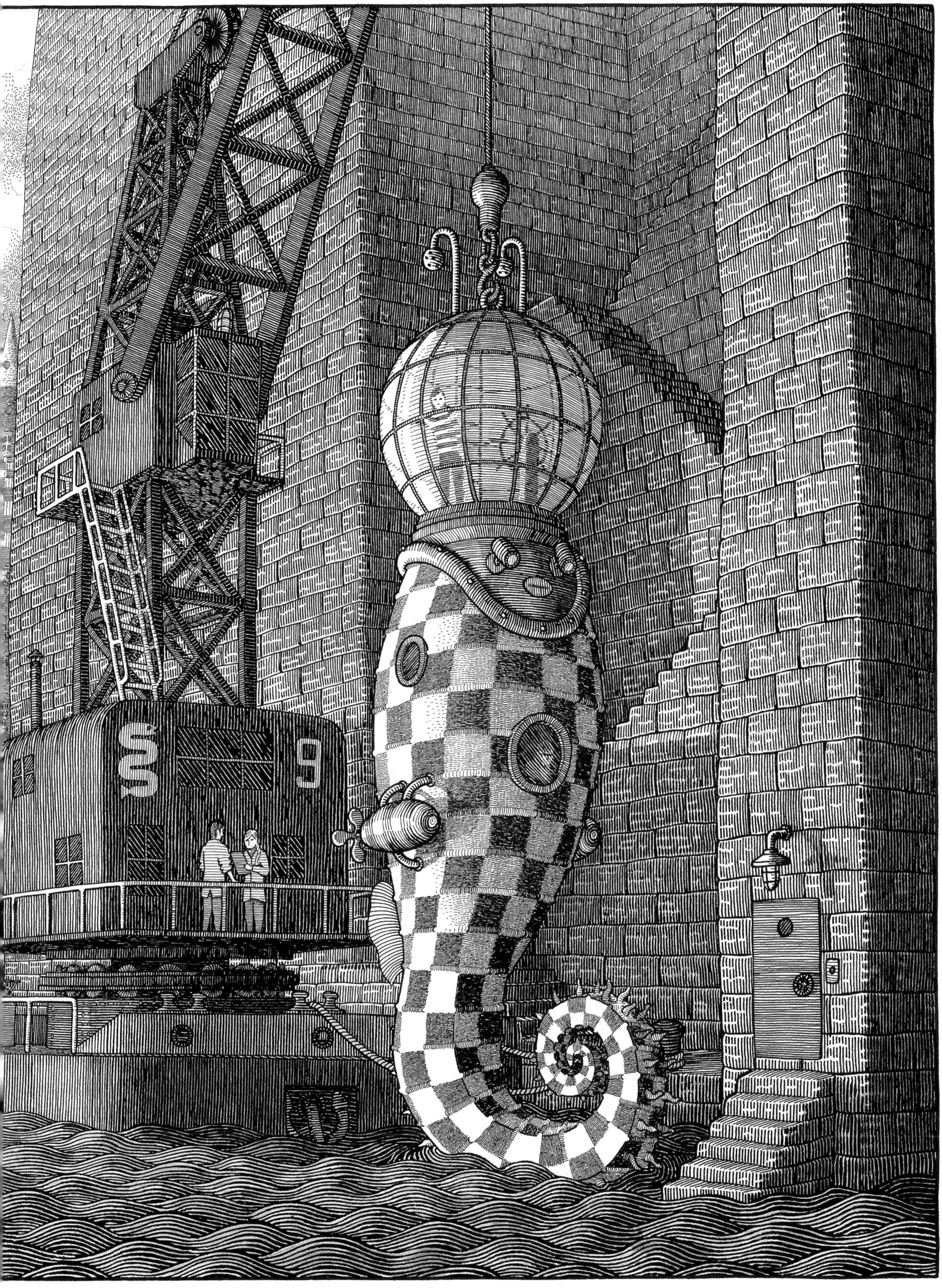

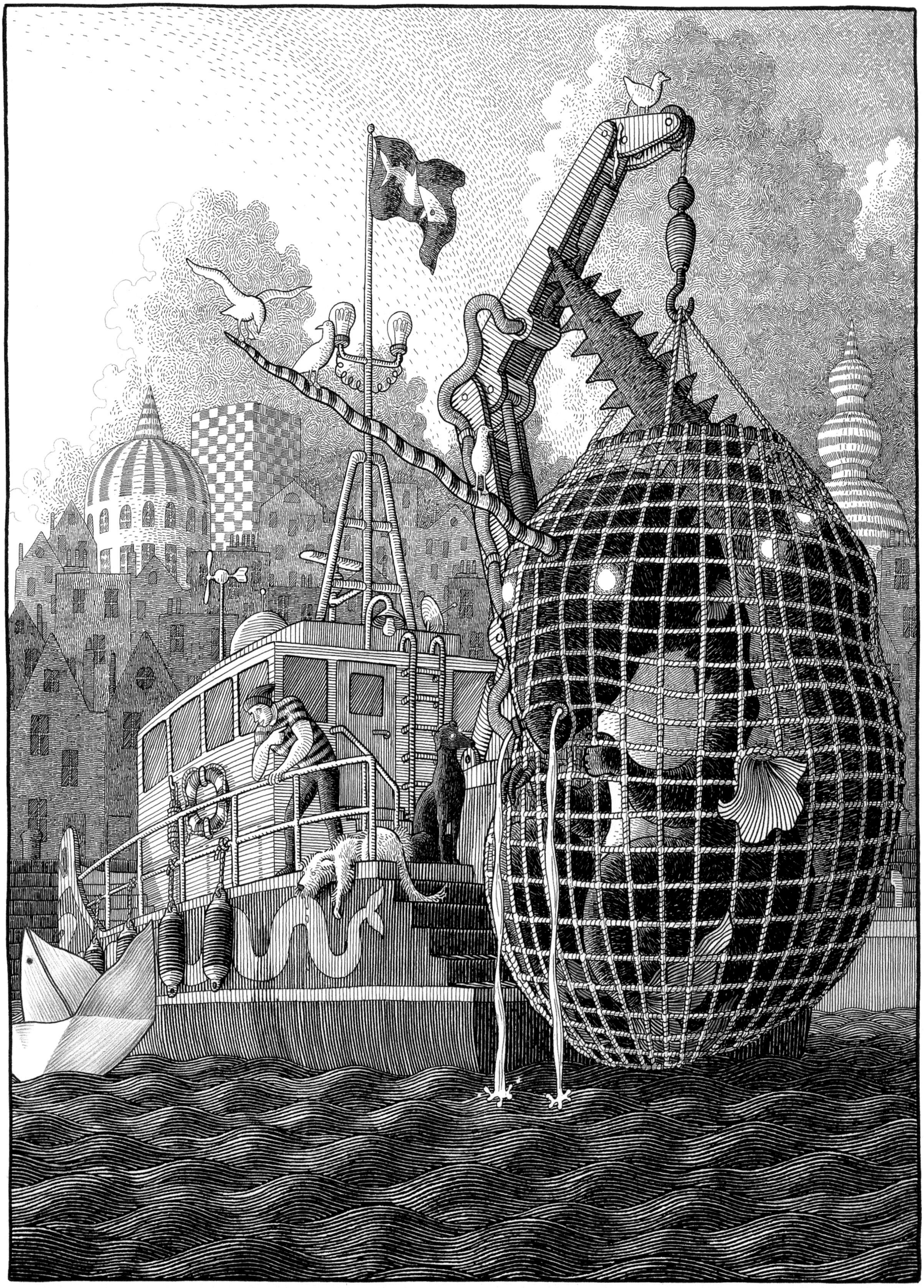

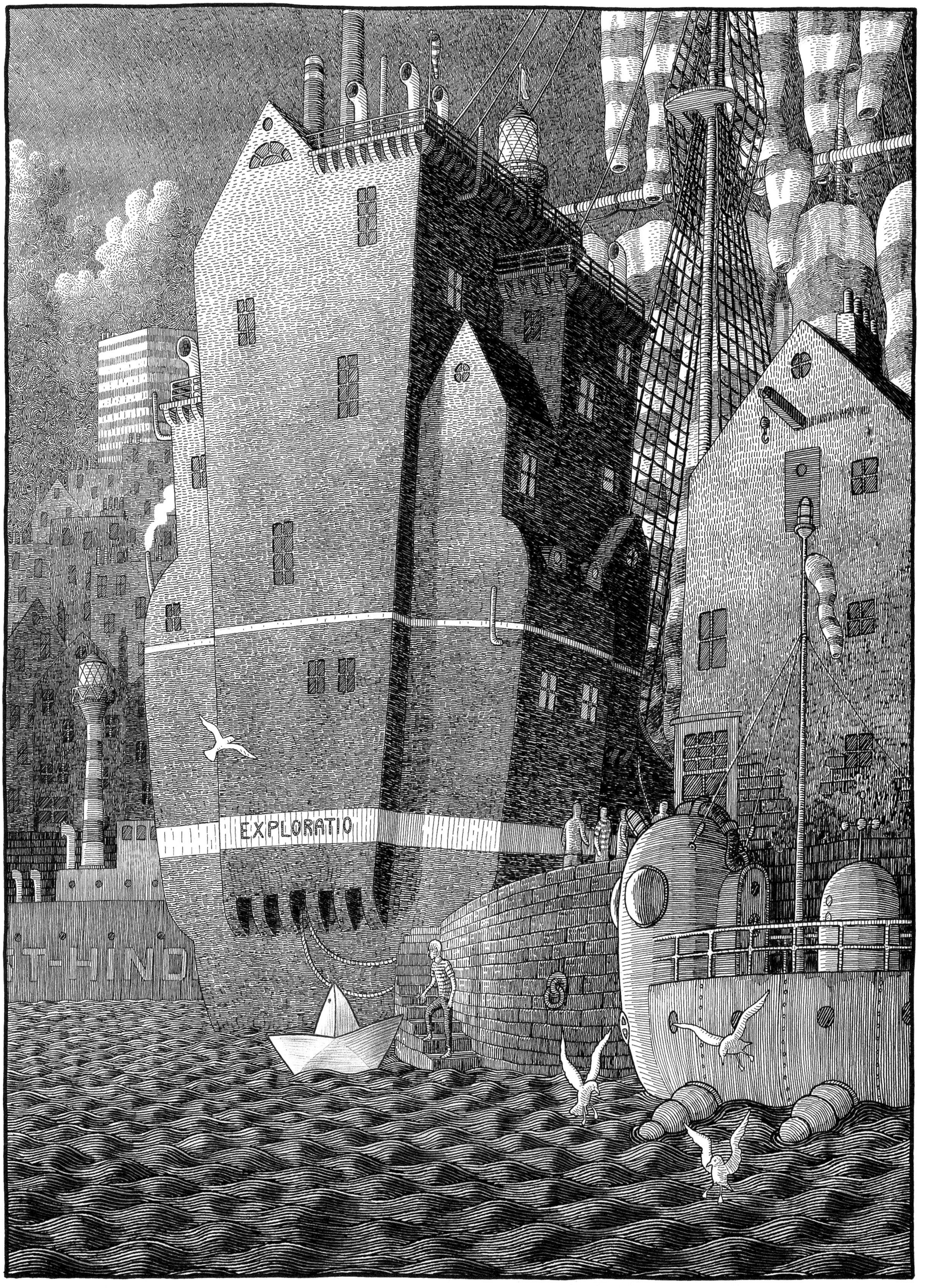
EXPLORATIO

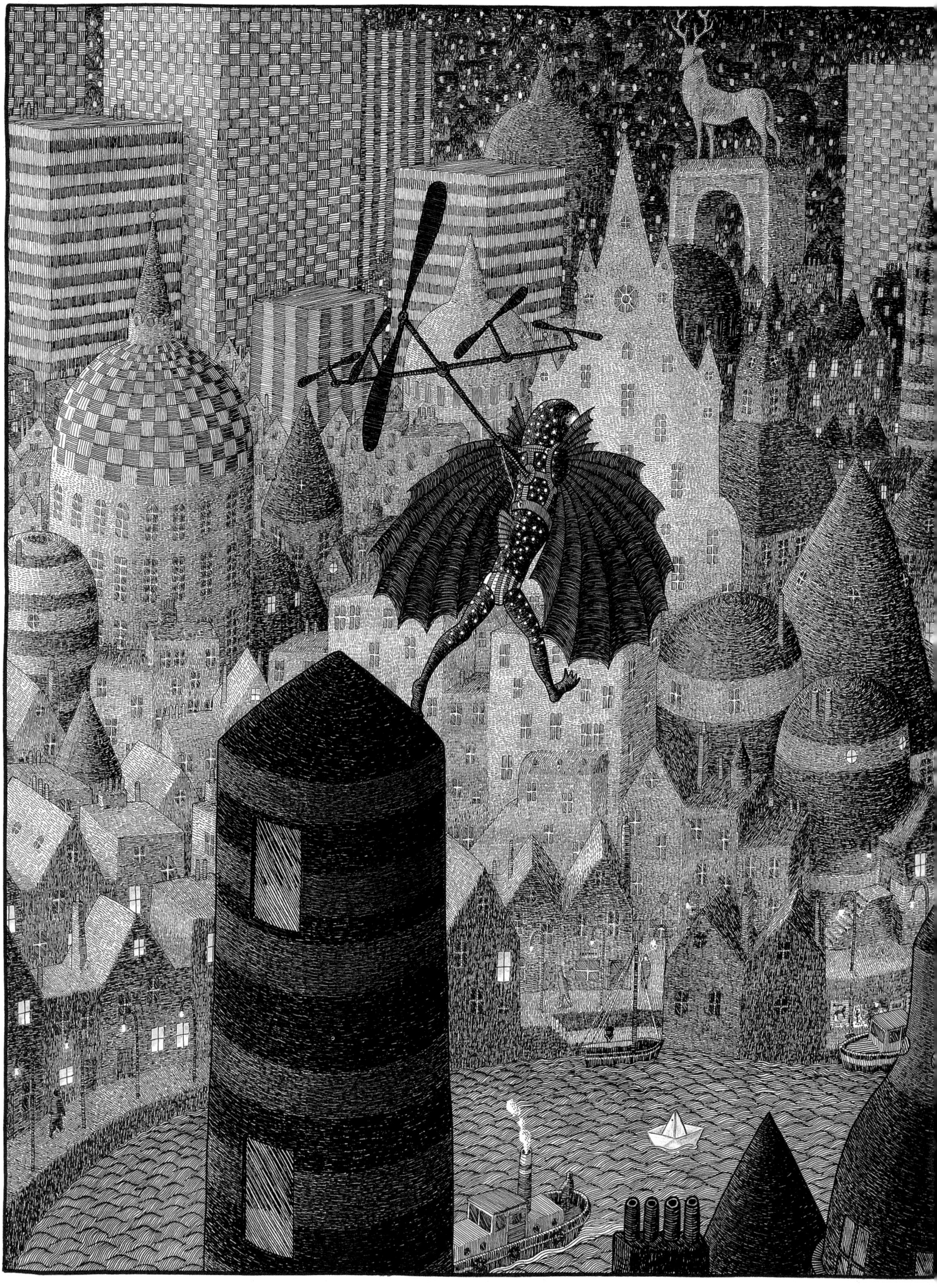

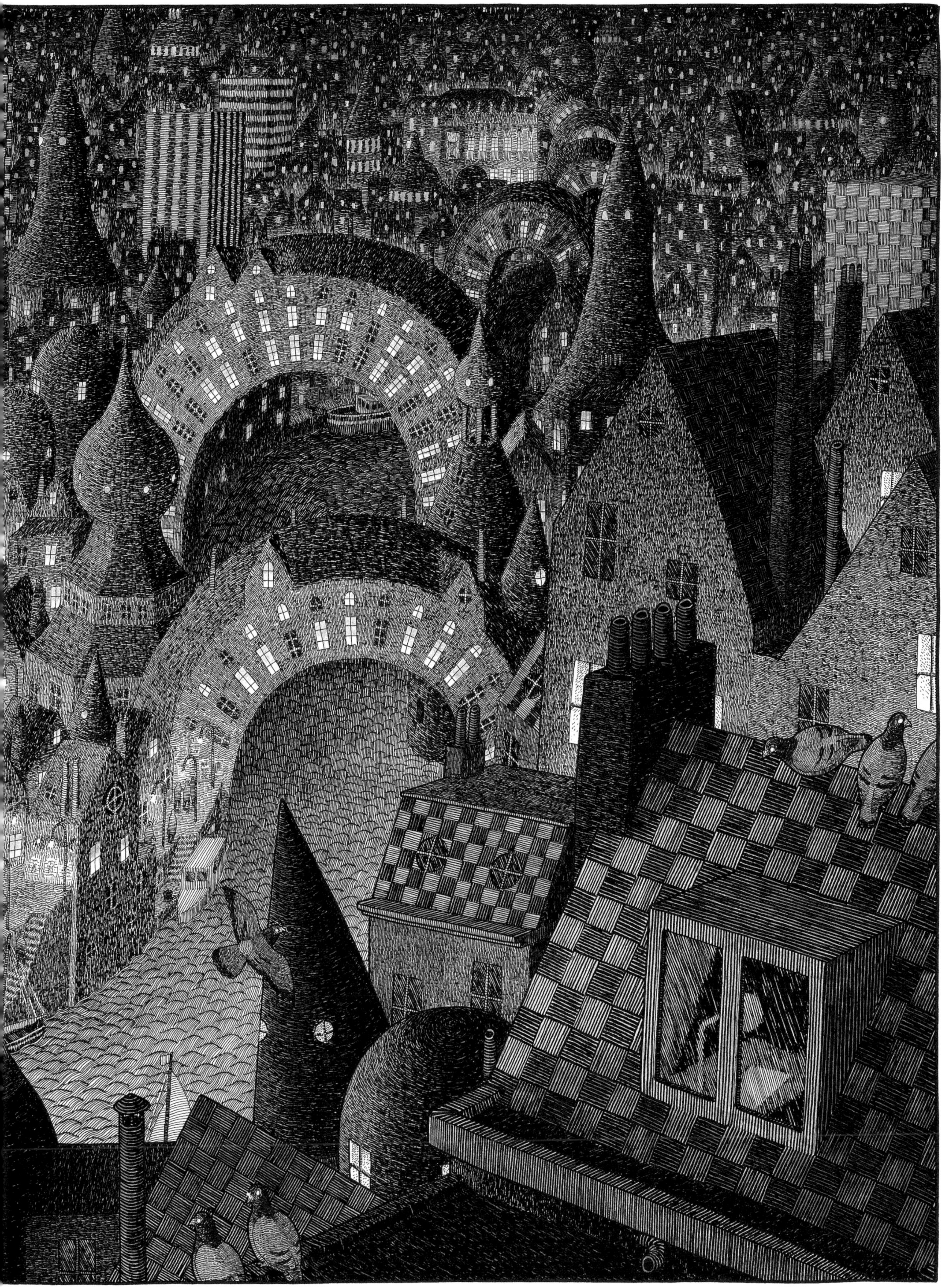

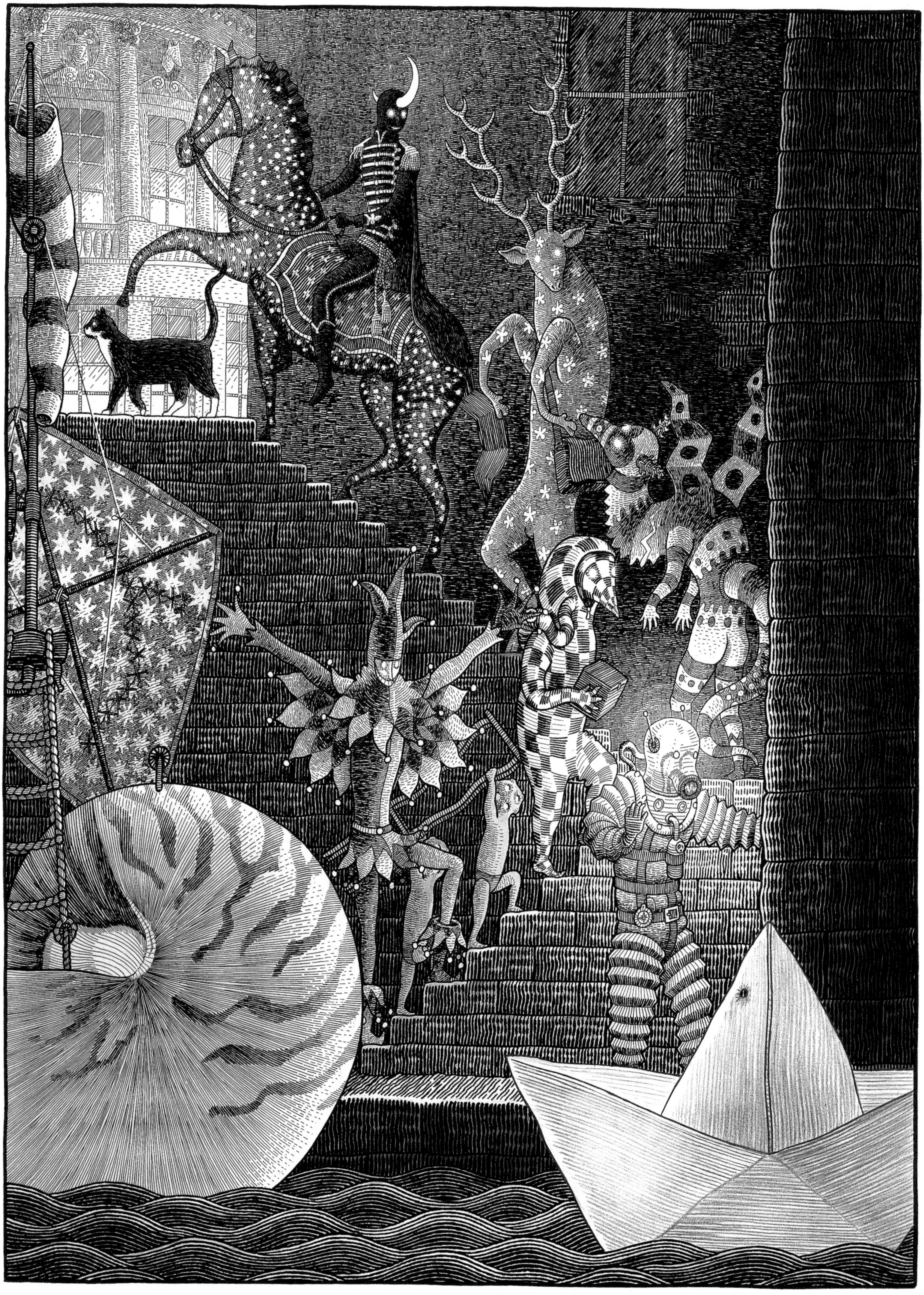

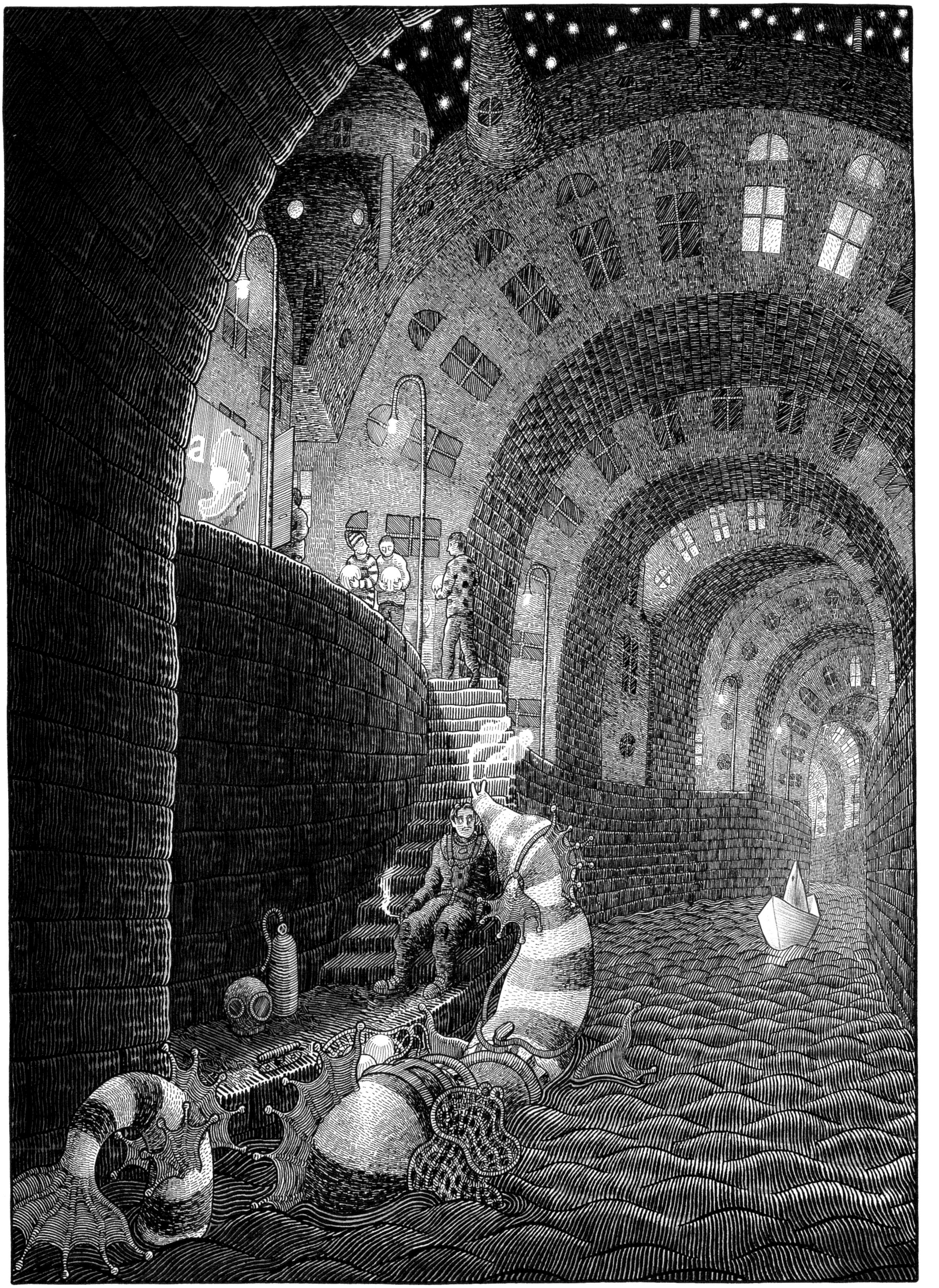

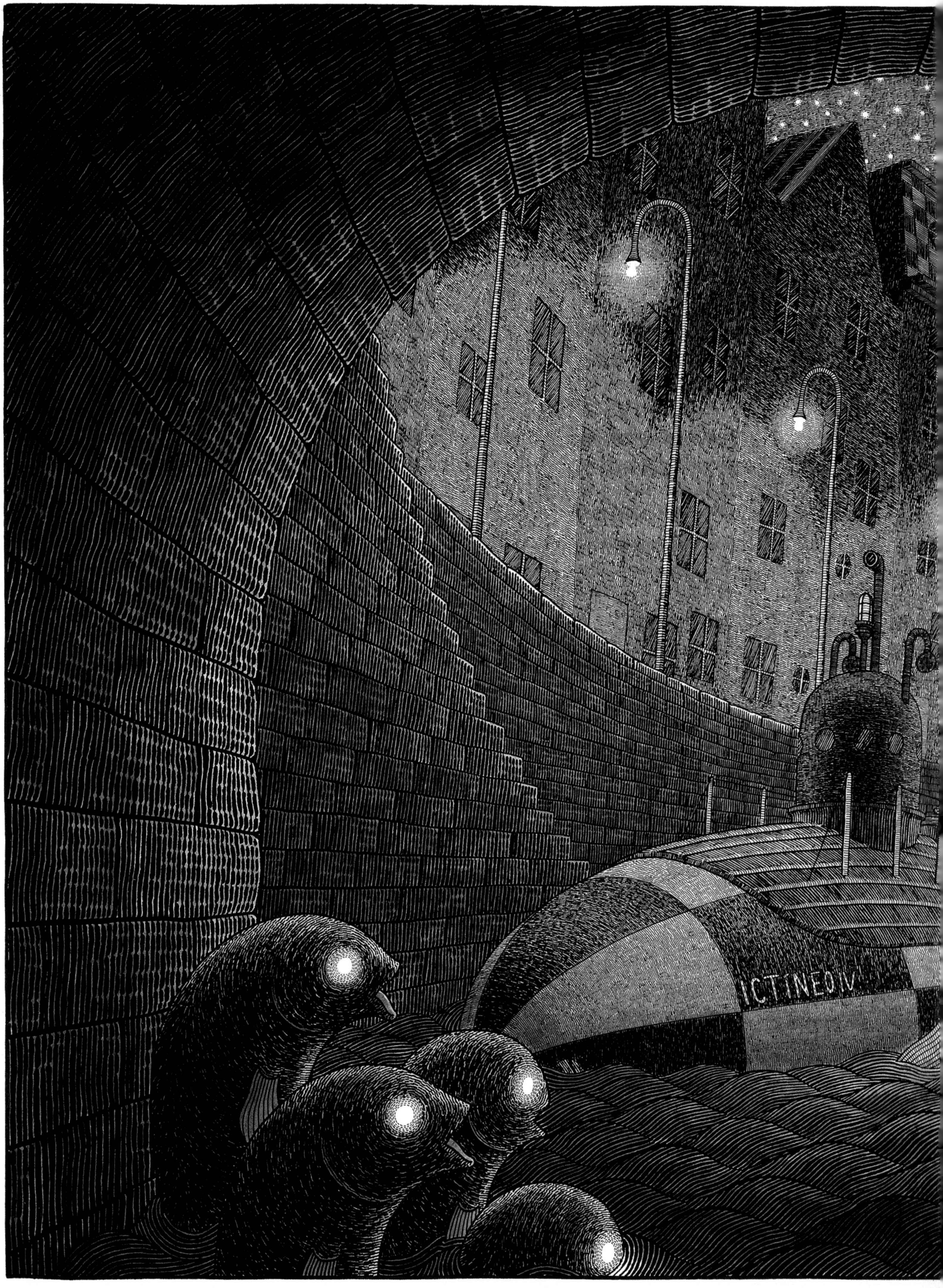
ICTINEO IV

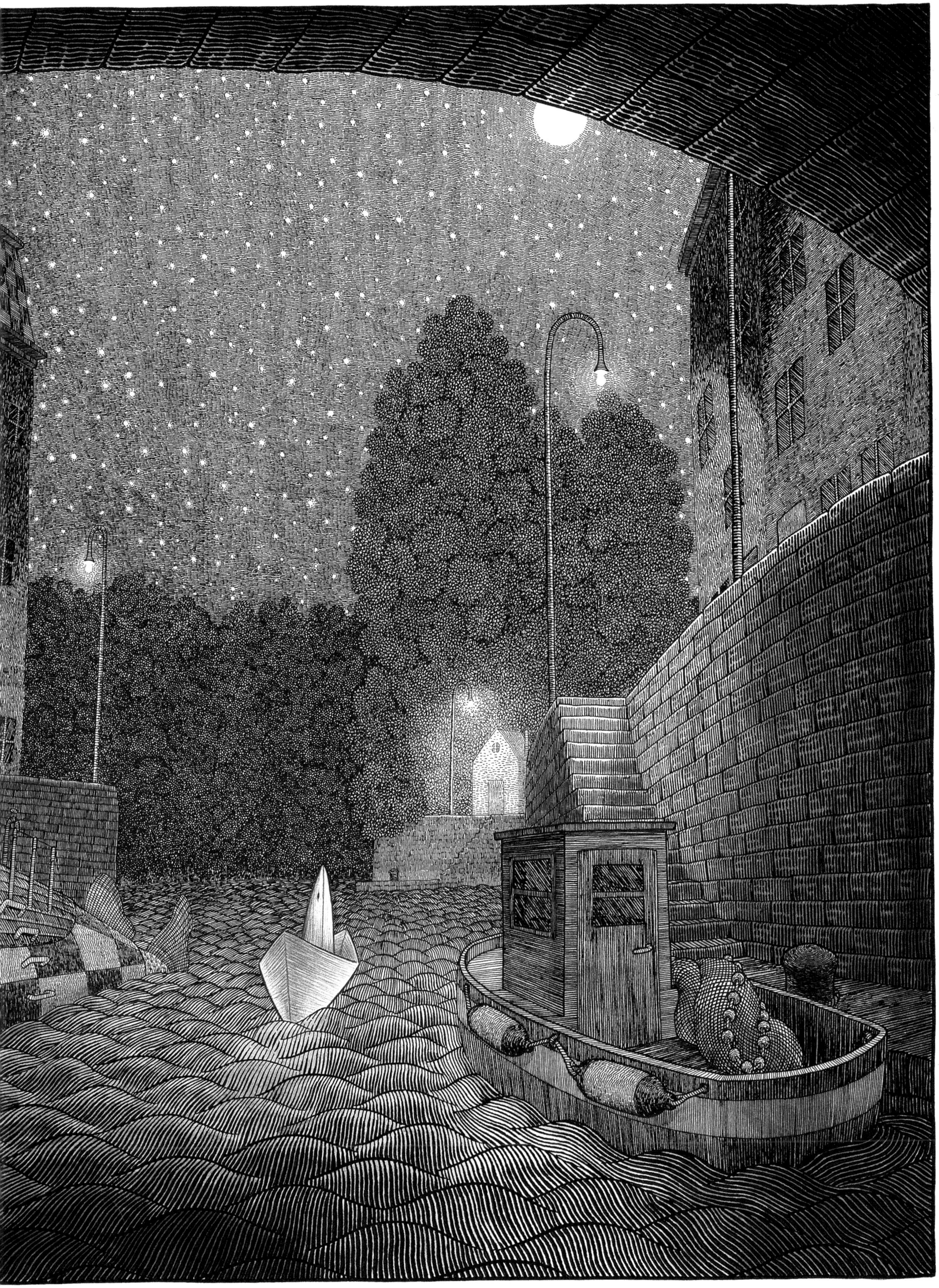

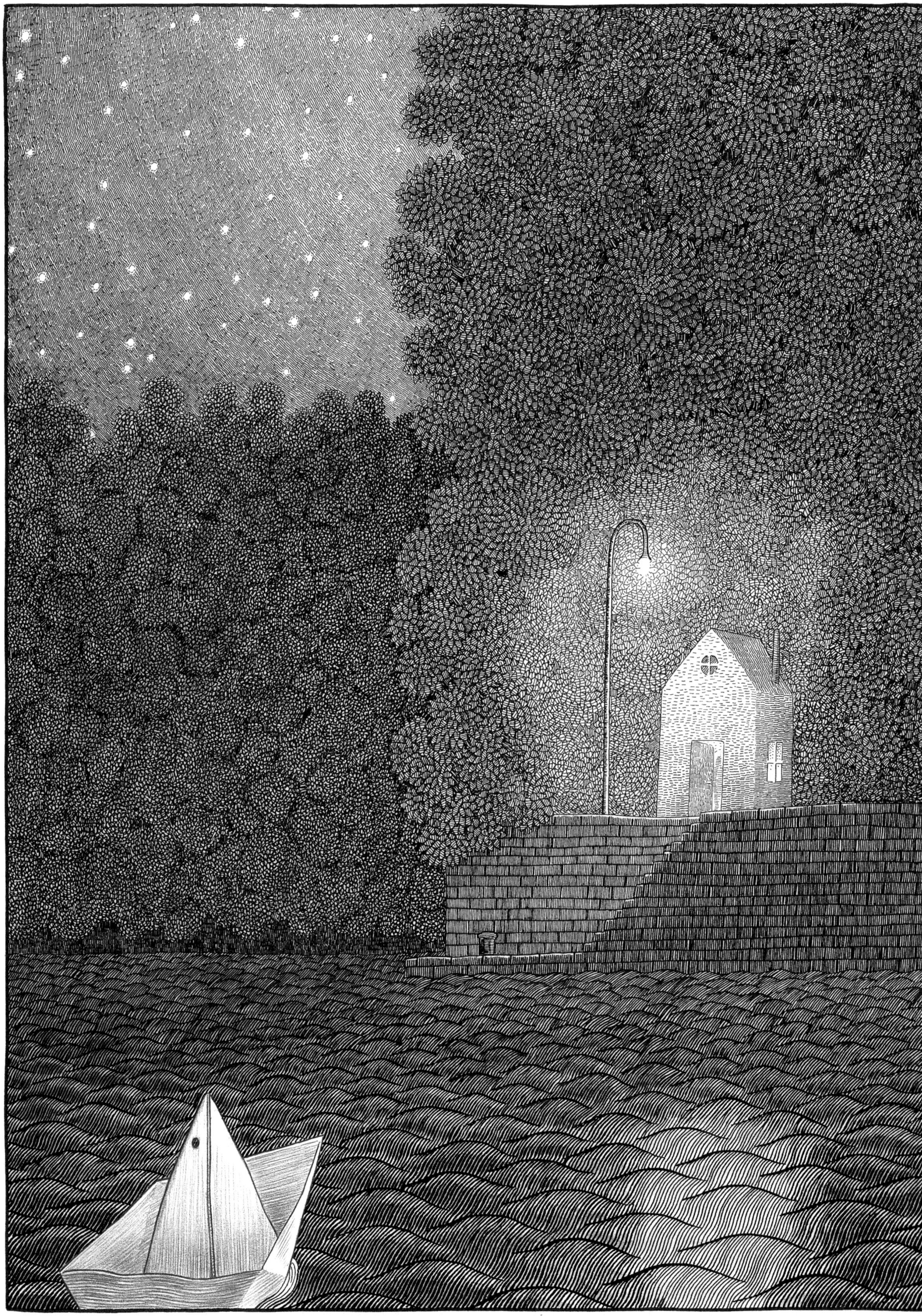

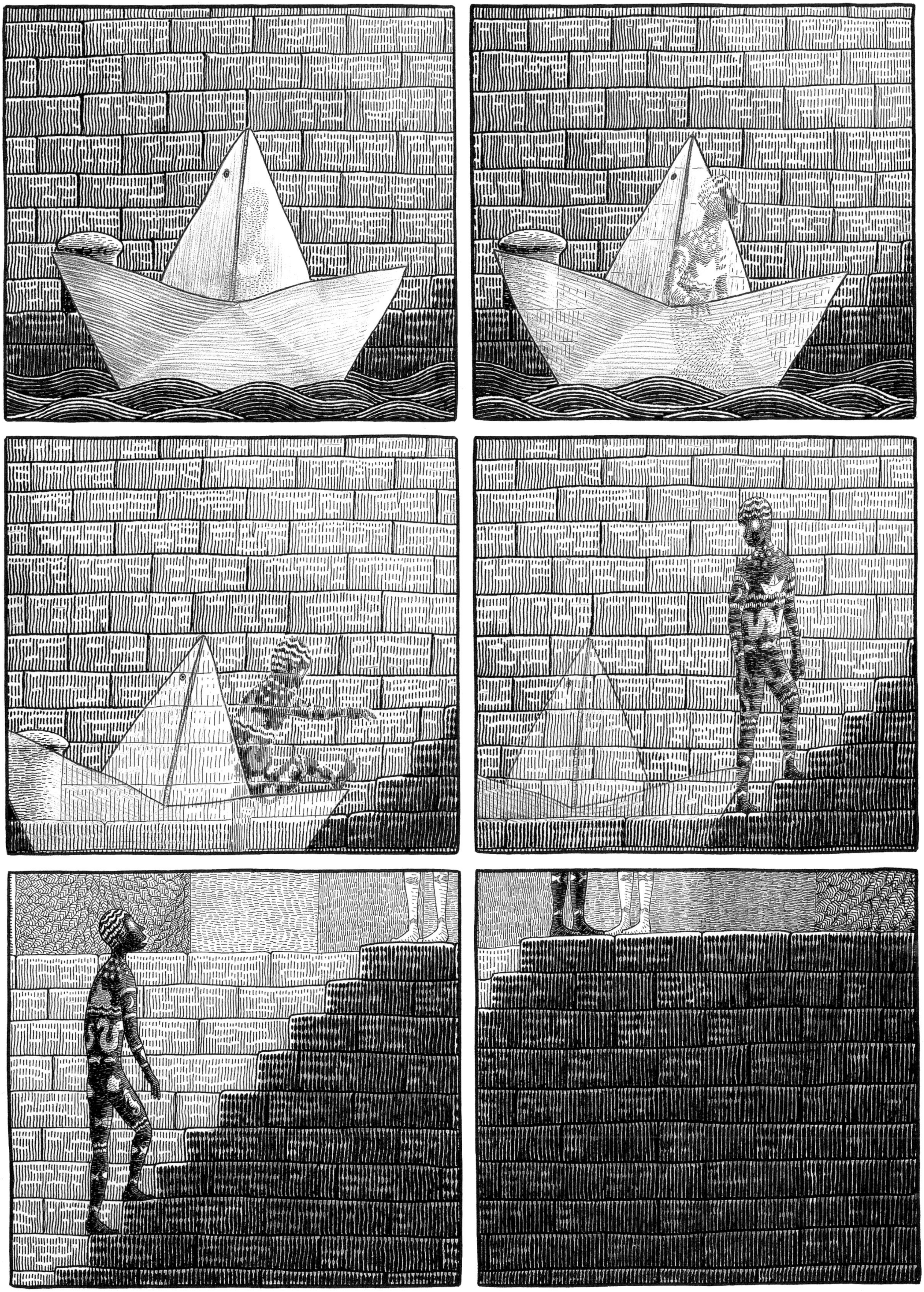

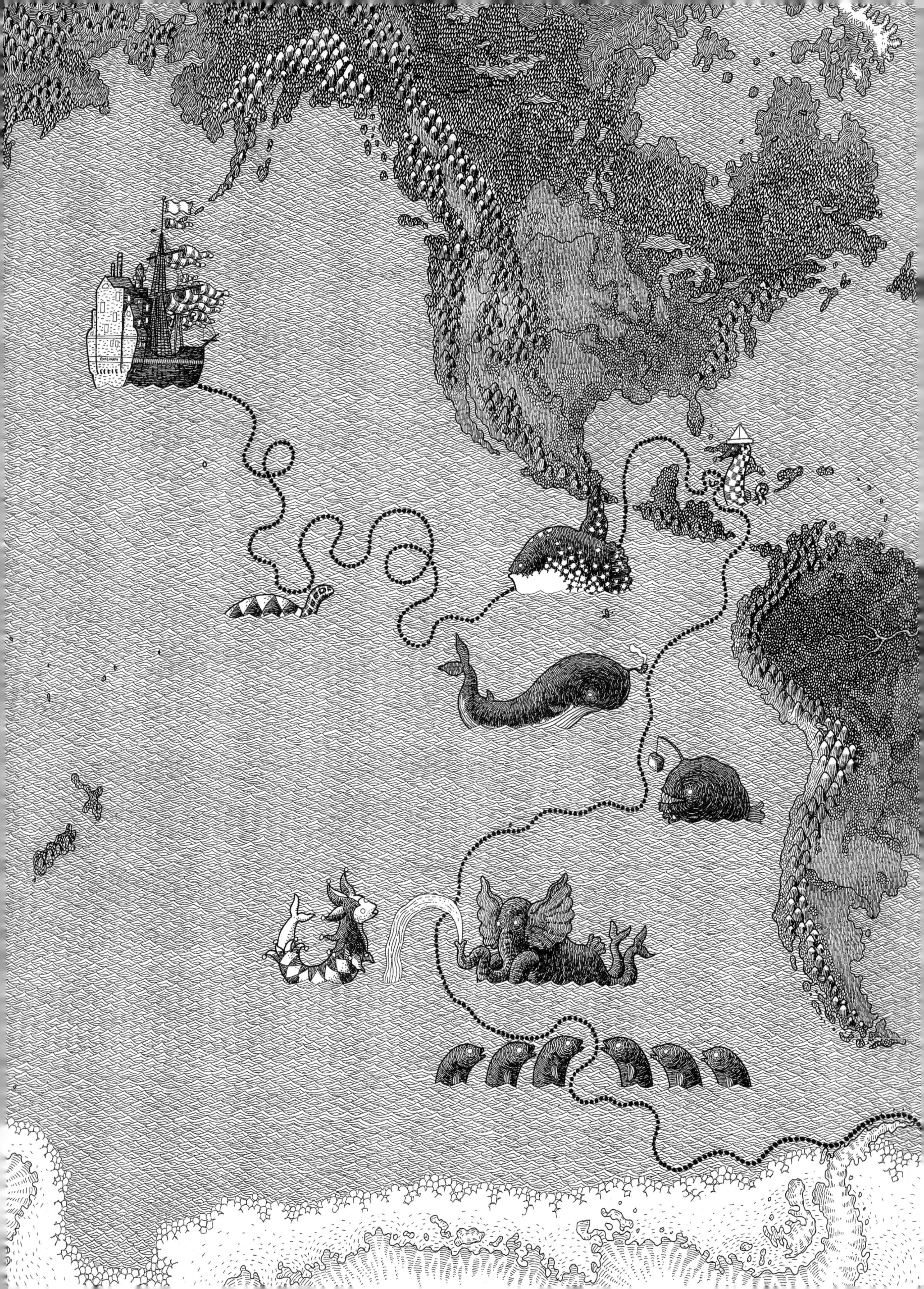